SELMA LAGERLÖF (1858-1940) was born on a farm in Värmland, trained as a teacher and became, in her life-time, Sweden's most widely translated author ever. Novels such as *Gösta Berlings saga* (1891; *Gösta Berling's Saga*) and *Jerusalem* (1901-02) helped regenerate Swedish literature, and the school reader, *Nils Holgersson's Wonderful Journey through Sweden* (1906-07), has achieved enduring international fame and popularity. Two very different trilogies, the Löwensköld trilogy (1925-28) and the Mårbacka trilogy (1922-32), the latter often taken to be autobiographical, give some idea of the range and power of Lagerlöf's writing. Several of her texts inspired innovative films, among them *Herr Arnes pengar* (*Sir Arne's Treasure*), directed by Mauritz Stiller (1919) and based on *Herr Arnes penningar* (1903; *Lord Arne's Silver)*, and *Körkarlen* (*The Phantom Carriage*), directed by Victor Sjöström (1921) and based on Lagerlöf's *Körkarlen* (1912). She was awarded the Nobel Prize for Literature, as the first woman ever, in 1909, and elected to the Swedish Academy, again as the first woman, in 1914. Having been able to buy back the farm of Mårbacka, which her family had lost as the result of bankruptcy, Lagerlöf spent the last three decades of her life combining her writing with the responsibilities for running a sizeable estate. Her work has been translated into close to 50 languages.

PETER GRAVES has translated works by Linnaeus, Jacob Wallenberg, August Strindberg, Selma Lagerlöf and Peter Englund, and he has been awarded a number of translation prizes. Before retiring he was Head of the School of Literatures, Languages and Cultures at the University of Edinburgh, where he taught Swedish.

Some other books from Norvik Press

August Strindberg: *Tschandala* (translated by Peter Graves)
August Strindberg: *The Red Room* (translated by Peter Graves)
August Strindberg: *The People of Hemsö* (translated by Peter Graves)
August Strindberg: *Strindberg's One-Act Plays* (Translated by Agnes Broomé, Anna Holmwood, John K Mitchinson, Mathelinda Nabugodi, Anna Tebelius and Nichola Smalley)
August Strindberg: *The Defence of a Madman* (translated by Carol Sanders and Janet Garton)

Kerstin Ekman: *Witches' Rings* (translated by Linda Schenck)
Kerstin Ekman: *The Spring* (translated by Linda Schenck)
Kerstin Ekman: *The Angel House* (translated by Sarah Death)
Kerstin Ekman: *City of Light* (translated by Linda Schenck)

P. C. Jersild: *A Living Soul* (translated by Rika Lesser)

Selma Lagerlöf: *Lord Arne's Silver* (translated by Sarah Death)
Selma Lagerlöf: *The Löwensköld Ring* (translated by Linda Schenck)
Selma Lagerlöf: *Charlotte Löwensköld* (translated by Linda Schenck)
Selma Lagerlöf: *The Phantom Carriage* (translated by Peter Graves)
Selma Lagerlöf: *Nils Holgersson's Wonderful Journey through Sweden* (translated by Peter Graves)

Hjalmar Söderberg: *Martin Birck's Youth* (translated by Tom Ellett)
Hjalmar Söderberg: *Selected Stories* (translated by Carl Lofmark)

Elin Wägner: *Penwoman* (translated by Sarah Death)

A Manor House Tale

by

Selma Lagerlöf

Translated from the Swedish
and with an
Afterword by Peter Graves

Series Preface by Helena Forsås-Scott

Norvik Press
2015

Originally published as *En herrgårdssägen* in 1899.

Norvik Press Series B: English Translations of Scandinavian Literature, no. 67

A catalogue record for this book is available from the British Library.

ISBN: 978-1-909408-25-8

Norvik Press gratefully acknowledges the generous support of the Anglo-Swedish Literary Foundation towards the publication of this translation.

Norvik Press
Department of Scandinavian Studies
University College London
Gower Street
London WC1E 6BT
United Kingdom
Website: www.norvikpress.com
E-mail address: norvik.press@ucl.ac.uk

Managing editors: Sarah Death, Helena Forsås-Scott, Janet Garton, C. Claire Thomson.

Cover design and layout: Marita Fraser

Contents

Series Preface

In the first comprehensive biography of the Swedish author Selma Lagerlöf (1858-1940), Elin Wägner has provided a snapshot of her at the age of 75 that gives some idea of the range of her achievements and duties. Sitting at her desk in the library at Mårbacka with its collection of classics from Homer to Ibsen, Lagerlöf is also able to view several shelves of translations of her books. Behind her she has not only her own works and studies of herself but also a number of wooden trays into which her mail is sorted. And the trays have labels like 'Baltic Countries, Belgium, Holland, Denmark, Norway, England, France, Italy, Finland, Germany, Sweden, Switzerland, the Slavic Countries, Austria-Hungary, Bonnier [her Swedish publisher], Langen [her German publisher], Swedish Academy, the Press, Relatives and Friends, Treasures, Mårbacka Oatmeal, Miscellaneous Duties'. Lagerlöf's statement, made to her biographer Elin Wägner a few years previously, that she had at least contributed to attracting tourists to her native province of Värmland, was clearly made tongue-in-cheek.

How could Selma Lagerlöf, a woman born into an upper-middle-class family in provincial Sweden around the middle of the nineteenth century, produce such an *œuvre* (sixteen novels, seven volumes of short stories) and achieve such status and fame in her lifetime?

Growing up on Mårbacka, a farm in the province of Värmland, at a time when the Swedish economy was predominantly agricultural, Selma Lagerlöf and her sisters learnt about the tasks necessary to keep the self-sufficient household ticking over, but their opportunities of getting an education beyond that which could be provided by their governess were close to non-existent. Selma Lagerlöf succeeded in borrowing money to spend three years in Stockholm training to become a teacher, one of the few professions open to women at the time, and after qualifying in 1885 she spent ten years teaching at a junior high school for girls in Landskrona, in the south of Sweden. Mårbacka had to be sold at auction in 1888, and Lagerlöf only resigned from her teaching post four years after the publication of her first novel, establishing herself as a writer in a Sweden quite different from the one in which she had grown up. Industrialisation in Sweden was late but swift, and Lagerlöf's texts found new readers among the urban working class.

Lagerlöf remained a prolific author well into the 1930s, publishing chiefly novels and short stories as well as a reader for school children, and she soon also gained recognition in the form of honours and prizes: an Honorary Doctorate at the University of Uppsala in 1907, the Nobel Prize for Literature, as the first woman, in 1909, and election to the Swedish Academy, again as the first woman, in 1914. Suffrage for women was only introduced in Sweden in 1919, and Lagerlöf became a considerable asset to the campaign. She was also able to repurchase Mårbacka, including the farm land, and from 1910 onwards she combined her work as a writer with the responsibility for a sizeable estate with a considerable number of employees.

To quote Lagerlöf's most recent biographer, Vivi Edström, she 'knew how to tell a story without ruining it'; but her innovative literary language with its close affinity with the spoken language required hard work and much experimentation. 'We authors', Lagerlöf wrote in a letter in 1908, 'regard a book as close to completion once we have found the style in which it allows itself to be written'.

Her first novel, *Gösta Berlings saga* (1891; *Gösta Berling's Saga*), was indeed a long time in the making as Lagerlöf experimented with genres and styles before settling for an exuberant and innovative form of prose fiction that is richly intertextual and frequently addresses the reader. Set in Värmland in the 1820s with the young and talented Gösta

Berling as the hero, the narrative celebrates the parties, balls and romantic adventures throughout 'the year of the cavaliers' at the iron foundry of Ekeby. But it does so against the backdrop of the expulsion of the Major's Wife who has been the benefactress of the cavaliers; and following her year-long pilgrimage and what has effectively been a year of misrule by the cavaliers, it is hard work and communal responsibility that emerge as the foundations of the future.

In *Drottningar i Kungahälla* (1899; *The Queens of Kungahälla*) Lagerlöf brought together a series of short stories and an epic poem set in Viking-age Kungälv, some distance north of Gothenburg, her aim being to explore some of the material covered by the medieval Icelandic author Snorri Sturluson in *Heimskringla*, but from the perspectives of the female characters. The terse narrative of *Herr Arnes penningar* (1903; *Lord Arne's Silver*), set in the sixteenth century in a context that highlights boundary crossings and ambivalences, has a plot revolving around murder and robbery, ghosts, love and eventual punishment. The slightly earlier short novel *En herrgårdssägen* (1899; *The Tale of a Manor*) similarly transcends boundaries as it explores music and dreams, madness and sanity, death and life in the context of the emerging relationship between a young woman and a man.

A few lines in a newspaper inspired Lagerlöf to her biggest literary project since *Gösta Berling's Saga*, the two-volume novel *Jerusalem* (1901-02), which also helped pave the way for her Nobel Prize later in the decade. The plot launches straight into the topic of emigration, prominent in Sweden since the 1860s, by exploring a farming community in the province of Dalarna and the emigration of part of the community to Jerusalem. The style was inspired by the medieval Icelandic sagas, but although the focus on emigration also establishes a thematic link with the sagas, the inversions of saga patterns such as bloody confrontations and family feuds become more prominent as the plot foregrounds peaceful achievements and international understanding. Yet this is first and foremost a narrative in which traditional structures of stability are torn apart, in which family relationships and relations between lovers are tried and often found wanting, and in which the eventual reconciliation between old and new comes at a considerable price.

Lagerlöf had been commissioned to write a school reader in 1901, but it was several years before she hit on the idea of presenting the geography, economy, history and culture of the provinces of Sweden through the narrative about a young boy criss-crossing the country on the back of a goose. While working on *Nils Holgerssons underbara resa genom Sverige* (1906-07; *Nils Holgersson's Wonderful Journey through Sweden*), Lagerlöf doubted that the text would find readers outside Sweden; paradoxically, however, *Nils Holgersson* was to become her greatest international success. Once perceived as an obstacle to the ambitions to award Lagerlöf the Nobel Prize for Literature, *Nils Holgersson* is nowadays read as a complex and innovative novel.

Körkarlen (1912; *The Phantom Carriage*) grew out of a request from The National Tuberculosis Society, and what was intended as a short story soon turned into a novel. The narrative about a victim of TB, whose death on New Year's Eve destines him to drive the death-cart throughout the following year and who only gains the respite to atone for his failures and omissions thanks to the affection and love of others, became the basis in 1921 for one of the best-known Swedish films of the silent era, with Victor Sjöström as the director (Sjöström also played the central character) and with ground-breaking cinematography by J. Julius (Julius Jaenzon).

The First World War was a difficult time for Lagerlöf. While many of her readers, in Sweden and abroad, were expecting powerful statements against the war, she felt that the political events were draining her creative powers. *Kejsarn av Portugallien* (1914; *The Emperor of Portugallia*) is not just a novel about the miracle of a newborn child and a father's love of his daughter; it is also a text about a fantasy world emerging in response to extreme external pressures, and about the insights and support this seemingly mad world can generate. Jan, the central character, develops for himself an outsider position similar to that occupied by Sven Elversson in Lagerlöf's more emphatically pacifist novel *Bannlyst* (1918; *Banished*), a position that allows for both critical and innovative perspectives on society.

Quite different from Lagerlöf's war-time texts, the trilogy consisting of *Löwensköldska ringen* (1925; *The Löwensköld Ring)*, *Charlotte Löwensköld* (1925) and *Anna Svärd* (1928) is at once lighthearted and serious, a narrative *tour de force* playing on ambivalences and multiple interpretations to an extent that has the potential to destabilise, in retrospect, any hard and fast readings of Lagerlöf's *œuvre*. As the trilogy calls into question the ghost of the old warrior General Löwensköld and then traces the demise of Karl-Artur Ekenstedt, a promising young minister in the State Lutheran Church, while giving prominence to a series of strong and independent female characters, the texts explore and celebrate the capacity and power of narrative.

Lagerlöf wrote another trilogy late in her career, and one that has commonly been regarded as autobiographical: *Mårbacka* (1922), *Ett barns memoarer* (1930; *Memories of My Childhood*), and *Dagbok för Selma Ottilia Lovisa Lagerlöf* (1932; *The Diary of Selma Lagerlöf*). All three are told in the first person; and with their tales about the Lagerlöfs, relatives, friends, local characters and the activities that structured life at Mårbacka in the 1860s and 70s, the first two volumes can certainly be read as evoking storytelling in the family circle by the fire in the evening. The third volume, *Diary*, was initially taken to be the authentic diary of a fourteen-year-old Selma Lagerlöf. Birgitta Holm's psychoanalytical study of Lagerlöf's work (1984) read the Mårbacka trilogy in innovative terms and singled out *Diary* as providing the keys to Lagerlöf's œuvre. Ulla-Britta Lagerroth has interpreted the trilogy as a gradual unmasking of patriarchy; but with 'Selma Lagerlöf' at its centre, this work can also be read as a wide-ranging and playful exploration of gender, writing and fame.

With the publication over the past couple of decades of several volumes of letters by Lagerlöf, to her friend Sophie Elkan (1994), to her mother (1998), to her friend and assistant Valborg Olander (2006), and to her friends Anna Oom and

Elise Malmros (2009-10), our understanding of Lagerlöf has undoubtedly become more complex. While the focus of much of the early research on Lagerlöf's work was biographical, several Swedish studies centring on the texts were published in connection with the centenary of her birth in 1958. A new wave of Lagerlöf scholarship began to emerge in Sweden in the late 1990s, exploring areas such narrative, gender, genre, and aesthetics; and in the 1990s the translation, reception and impact of Lagerlöf's texts abroad became an increasingly important field, investigated by scholars in for example the US, the UK and Japan as well as in Sweden. Current research is expanding into the interrelations between a range of media in Lagerlöf, performance studies, cultural transmissions, and archival studies. As yet there is no scholarly edition of Lagerlöf, but thanks to the newly established Selma Lagerlöf Archive (Selma Lagerlöf-arkivet, SLA) a scholarly edition in digitised form is underway.

By the time Lagerlöf turned 80, in 1938, she was the most widely translated Swedish writer ever, and the total number of languages into which her work has been translated is now close to 50. However, most of the translations into English were made soon after the appearance of the original Swedish texts, and unlike the original texts, translations soon become dated. Moreover, as Peter Graves has concluded in a study of Lagerlöf in Britain, Lagerlöf 'was not well-served by her translators [into English]'. The Norvik Press series 'Lagerlöf in English' aims to remedy this situation.

Helena Forsås-Scott

I

It was a beautiful autumn day towards the end of the 1830s. In Uppsala at that time there was a tall, yellow, two-storied house that stood strangely alone on a small meadow right out on the edge of the town. It was a rather shabby and unattractive house, but its saving grace was the mass of Virginia creeper that grew so high up the yellow wall on the sunny side that it completely surrounded the three windows on the upper floor.

In the room behind one of those windows a student sat drinking his morning coffee. He was a tall handsome fellow with fine features. He wore his curly hair swept straight back from his forehead, though he had a fringe that constantly threatened to fall over his eyes. He was dressed in comfortable and casual clothes, but was quite elegant for all that.

His room was well-furnished with a good sofa and padded chairs, a large desk and splendid bookcases, but there were hardly any books.

Before he had finished his coffee, another student came in and joined him. He was a very different sort of person, a short, broad-shouldered fellow, stocky and strong, ugly, with a big face, thin hair and coarse skin.

'Hede,' he said, 'I have come to have a serious talk with you.'

'Are you in some sort of trouble?'

'Oh no, not me,' the other replied, 'you're the one it's all about, not me.' He sat in silence for a while, looking down. 'It's damned unpleasant for me to have to say it!'

'Don't bother then!' Hede suggested. The earnest solemnity of all this made him want to laugh.

'I can't put it off any longer,' his visitor said. 'I ought to have spoken long ago but it's not really my place, you know. I can't help thinking that you must be sitting there saying to yourself: there goes Gustav Ålin, son of one of my crofters, and now he thinks he's the man to put me straight.'

'For Heaven's sake, Ålin, don't imagine I'm thinking anything of the kind,' Hede said. 'After all, my grandfather was a farmer's son, wasn't he?'

'Yes, but no one remembers that any longer,' Ålin said. And he sat there in front of Hede, heavy and dull, falling back more and more into a rustic manner as if that would help him out of his embarrassment.

'Look here now, given the difference between your family and mine I think I should hold my tongue, but when I remember that it was your father who in his day helped me and made it possible for me to be a student, I think that I ought to speak.'

Hede looked at him with a pleasant twinkle in his eyes.

'Speak then, and get all these worries off your chest!' he said.

'It's like this,' Ålin said, 'I hear people talk and they say that you are doing nothing. They say you've hardly opened a book in the four terms you've been at this university. They say that all you do is play the fiddle all day, and I think that's more than likely since it's all you wanted to do even when you were at school in Falun. Though they did make you work when you were there.'

Hede shifted rather awkwardly in his chair. Ålin became more and more unhappy, but he went on resolutely:

'I've no doubt you think that someone who owns an estate like Munkhyttan should be able to do what he likes – work if he wants to, do nothing if he wants to. If he takes an exam, that's good. If he doesn't take an exam, that's almost as good, because you don't want to be anything other than the proprietor of the Munkhyttan estate anyway. You want to live there for the whole of your life. That's the way you think, I know that, I really do.'

Hede said nothing and he seemed to Ålin to be enclosed within the same kind of wall of superiority that had surrounded Hede's father, the inspector of mines, and his mother.

'There is no doubt that Munkhyttan is not what it used to be when the iron mine was productive,' Ålin continued cautiously. 'And there is no doubt that your father knew that, which is why he decided before his death that you should study something. Your poor mother knows it too, as does the whole parish. The only one who seems ignorant of it is you, Hede.'

'Are you suggesting,' Hede said with a touch of irritation, 'that I'm not aware that the mine is no longer workable?'

'No,' Ålin said, 'you certainly know that, but what you don't know is that it means the end of the Munkhyttan estate. Think about it and you'll see for yourself that it's impossible to live on agriculture alone in western Dalarna. Indeed, I don't know why your mother has kept it secret from you. But then, as the sole heritor she doesn't need to ask your advice about anything. Anyway, everyone back there knows that she's in straitened circumstances and has to go round borrowing money, so they say. She probably didn't want to bother you with her worries and thought she could keep everything going until after your exams. She doesn't want to sell the property until you have finished and have a new home.'

Hede got up and took a turn around the room before stopping in front of Ålin.

'What a fellow you are! Here you are, doing your very best to make me believe that rubbish. We are rich, you know, rich.'

'I'm well aware that your people are still regarded as grand back there. For the time being,' Ålin said. 'But surely you can understand that things can't continue with money going out and nothing coming in. It was quite different when you had the mine.'

Hede sat down again.

'My mother should have let me know about this, shouldn't she?' he said. 'I'm grateful to you, Ålin, but you've allowed wagging tongues and gossip to frighten you.'

'That's just as I thought,' Ålin continued doggedly, 'you didn't know anything about it. Back in Munkhyttan your mother is pinching and saving to get money to send to you in

Uppsala and to make sure things are jolly and cheerful when you are at home during the vacations. Meanwhile you are here doing nothing because you don't know the danger that is just round the corner. I simply couldn't carry on watching the way the two of you were deceiving one another. Your lady mother believed you were studying and you believed she was rich. I couldn't just stay silent and leave you to destroy your future.'

Hede sat in silence for a while, thinking. Then he stood up and with a sad smile held out his hand to Ålin.

'I'm sure you know that I realise you are telling the truth even though I don't want to believe you. Thank you!'

Ålin shook his hand, beaming with satisfaction.

'You do understand, don't you, Hede, that nothing is lost as long as you work? With a mind like yours you can finish your degree in seven or eight terms.'

Hede drew himself up to his full height.

'Have no fear, Ålin,' he said. 'I shall start working now.'

Ålin rose and walked towards the door more than a little hesitantly. Before reaching the threshold he turned round.

'I had something else in mind too,' he said, once again becoming acutely embarrassed. 'I want to ask you to lend me your fiddle until you really get into the swing of your studies.'

'Lend you my fiddle?'

'Yes, wrap it in the silk cloth, lock it in its case and let me take it away with me, otherwise you won't do any reading. I would no sooner be out of the door than you would be playing it. It's become such a habit that you wouldn't be able to resist if you still had it here. There's no way of overcoming something like that without help. It's stronger than you are.'

Hede was reluctant.

'That's just nonsense,' he said.

'Oh no, it most certainly isn't nonsense. You know, don't you, that you inherited it from your father? Playing the fiddle is in your blood. Ever since you came up to Uppsala and became your own master you have done nothing else. That's why you live out here on the edge of the town, isn't it, so that your playing won't disturb anyone else. You simply can't help yourself, so let me take the fiddle.'

'Well,' Hede said, 'in the past I wouldn't have been able to stop myself playing. But Munkhyttan is at stake now and I love my home more than I love my fiddle.'

Ålin, however, remained persistent and asked again for the fiddle.

'What is the point?' Hede asked. 'If I want to play I wouldn't have to go very far to borrow another fiddle.'

'I know that,' Ålin answered, 'but I don't think the risk would be so great with a different fiddle. It's this old Italian fiddle that poses the worst danger. And there is something else as well – I suggest you allow me to lock you in for the first few days. Just while you get properly started.'

But however much Ålin pleaded Hede resisted. He was not prepared to submit to anything so ridiculous as house arrest. Ålin's face flushed bright red.

'I have to take the fiddle with me,' he said, 'otherwise our whole conversation will have been pointless.' He continued in a heated and urgent tone: 'I didn't want to say anything about it but I know there is more than Munkhyttan at stake. I saw a girl at the graduation ball last spring and I was told she was engaged to you. I don't dance myself but it filled me with joy to see how lightly she danced and how she shone bright as a flower on the meadow. But when I heard she was engaged to you I felt so sorry for her.'

'Did you?'

'Yes, I certainly did, because I knew that you were going to make nothing of yourself if you continued as you had begun. And I swore an oath that the girl would be spared from spending her whole life waiting for someone who never came. She should not be left to sit and wither away waiting for you. I have no desire to meet her in a few years and see her with sharp features and deep wrinkles around her mouth …'

He broke off. Hede's eyes were gazing at him with a look of intense enquiry.

For Gunnar Hede had immediately realised that Ålin was fond of his fiancée and he was deeply touched that he would nevertheless want to save him. Influenced by this emotion,

Hede gave way and handed him his fiddle case.

Once Ålin had gone Hede read desperately for a whole hour before tossing the book aside.

What was the point of studying? It would take him three or four years to finish and who could guarantee that his property would not have been sold in the meantime?

With a feeling close to terror he realised how much he loved the old place. It held him in its spell and he could see every room and every tree in his mind's eye. His happiness depended on not losing any of those things.

And he was supposed to stick to his books while risking all that!

He grew more and more upset and could feel the blood pounding at his temples as if he were suffering from a fever. And not being able to pick up his fiddle and play himself calm made him feel utterly desperate.

'My God,' he said, 'that Ålin fellow will end up driving me mad. First of all he tells me these things and then robs me of my fiddle! Someone like me needs to feel a bow in his fingers both in sorrow and in joy. I must do something, I must get hold of money, but my mind is completely blank. I can't think without my fiddle.'

Hede was furious at being confined and told to apply himself to his books. It was madness to start working for an examination that was so far off when what he needed was money, money, money.

He found the sense of confinement intolerable. He was so angry with Ålin for coming up with these silly ideas that he was afraid he might strike him when he came back.

Oh yes, if he'd only had his fiddle he would most certainly have been playing it by now, that was exactly what he needed to be doing. He was so distressed that his blood was seething and he was on the verge of madness.

At the very moment Hede was longing for his fiddle, a wandering fiddler came by and began to play down in the yard below. He was a blind old man whose playing was out of tune and lacking in expression, but Hede was so entranced just to hear the sound of a fiddle that he listened with tears in his eyes and his hands clasped.

The very next instant he threw open his window and climbed down with the help of the Virginia creeper. Not a pang of conscience did he feel at leaving his work. He thought the fiddle had come to the house for no other purpose than to comfort him in his unhappiness.

Hede had probably never begged for anything as humbly as he now begged the blind old man to lend him his fiddle. He stood there cap in hand the whole time, even though the man was as blind as blind could be.

The old man did not seem to understand what was wanted and he turned to the girl who was leading him. Hede bowed to the poor lass and repeated his request. She looked at him in the way that someone whose eyes must act for two studies people. Her big grey eyes gazed at him so steadily that Hede thought he could feel her gaze physically: at one moment it rested on his neckband, checking that the ruffle was freshly starched, then it looked to see that his coat had been brushed, and then that his boots had been polished.

Hede had never before been subjected to such an inspection and it was obvious to him that those eyes would find him wanting.

But they did not. The girl had a peculiar way of smiling. Her face was so serious that when she did smile it looked as if it was the first and only time she had ever managed to look happy. And one of these rare smiles now came gliding over her lips.

She took the fiddle from the old man and handed it to Hede.

'Now we'll have the waltz from *Der Freischütz*,' she said.

Hede thought it strange that he should have to play a waltz just then, but it was all the same to him what he played as long as he had a bow in his hand.

That was all he needed. The fiddle immediately began to comfort him, speaking to him in weak, shrill tones.

'I'm just a poor man's fiddle,' it said, 'but such as I am, I bring help and comfort to a poor blind man. I am the light and the colour and the clarity in his life. I am the one who comforts him in his poverty and his old age and his blindness.'

Hede felt the dreadful depression that had been pressing down on all his hopes begin to lift.

'You are young and you are strong,' the fiddle said to him. 'You can fight and you can struggle. You can hold on firmly to the things that threaten to desert you. Why are you so dispirited and depressed?'

Hede had been playing with his eyes lowered, but now he threw back his head and looked at those around him. There was a small crowd of children and idlers from the street who had come into the yard to listen to the music.

But they had not come for the sake of the music alone, because there were other members of the troupe as well as the blind man and the girl.

Opposite Hede stood a figure in tights and sequins, his bare arms crossed over his chest. He looked old and worn, but Hede could not help thinking what a fine fellow he was with his broad chest and long moustaches. And there was his wife, small and fat and not particularly young either, but with a wide happy smile above her sequins and swaying gauze skirts.

At the first beats of the music they stood still and counted. Then with a gracious smile on their lips they took one another by the hand and danced on a small patchwork quilt.

And Hede noticed that during all the feats of equilibristics they now performed the wife remained almost motionless while her husband worked alone. He jumped over her, cartwheeled round her and somersaulted over her. His wife did almost nothing apart from blow kisses at the audience.

But Hede was not really thinking about them. His bow had begun to fly over the strings and it was telling him that happiness lies in fighting and in conquering. It seemed almost to be counting him fortunate to have everything at stake. Hede was playing for his own courage and hope and he was not thinking of the old acrobats.

But then suddenly he noticed that they were becoming restless. They stopped smiling and no more kisses were blown to the public. The acrobat leapt madly and his wife began to sway back and forth in waltz time.

Hede was playing more and more frantically. He moved on from *Der Freischütz* and threw himself into one of those age-old tunes associated with the magic of water sprites, the kind of melody that drives everyone crazy when they hear it played at a feast.

The old acrobats quite lost their heads, stood and waited in breathless amazement until a moment came when they were no longer able to resist. They sprang forward into each other's arms and began to dance the waltz in the middle of the patchwork quilt.

Oh, how they danced, how they danced! With small tripping steps and whirling in tight little circles, they scarcely stepped off the mat. Their faces shone with delight and ecstasy. The joy of youth and the giddiness of love had come over the old people.

All the people rejoiced to see them dance. A great smile spread over the face of the serious little girl who led the blind man and Hede himself was filled with wild excitement.

Just look at what his fiddle could achieve! It could take people right out of themselves! What great power he had at his command! He could take possession of his kingdom whenever he wanted.

A couple of years studying abroad with some great master and he would be ready to travel the world and earn money, honour and fame with his playing.

Hede felt that the acrobats had come there to tell him that, to show him a road that lay bright and open before him.

He said to himself: I shall be a musician, I shall be, I must be. It's better than studying. I can put a spell on people with my fiddle and I can become rich.

Hede stopped playing. The acrobats immediately stepped forward to compliment him.

The man told him his name was Blomgren. That was his real name, he used other names when he was performing. He and his wife were circus people and had been so for many years. Fru Blomgren had been known as Miss Viola in the days when she performed tricks on horseback. And even now, although they had left the circus, they were still artistes, passionate artistes. He must surely have noticed that already, hadn't he. That was why they had found it impossible to resist his fiddle.

Hede kept company with the acrobats for several hours. He could not part from the fiddle and he liked the passion these old performers felt for their calling. As for him, he was testing himself: 'I want to see if I have the stuff of the artist in me, I want to see if I can stir the passions, I want to see if I can make children and idlers follow me from one courtyard to another.'

As they walked between yards Herr Blomgren threw on a worn old greatcoat and Fru Blomgren wrapped herself in a round brown cape, and thus attired they walked beside Hede and chatted.

Herr Blomgren was reluctant to talk about all the honours that had been heaped upon him and Fru Blomgren during the time they had belonged to a real circus. But then the manager had dismissed Fru Blomgren on the pretext that she had become too corpulent. Herr Blomgren had not been dismissed, but he had asked to be paid what was due to him. Surely no one would have expected Herr Blomgren to continue working for a manager who had dismissed his wife?

Fru Blomgren loved her art and Herr Blomgren had decided to become an independent artiste so that she could continue performing. In winter, when it was too cold to work the street, they put on performances in a tent and they had a very rich repertoire of pantomime, conjuring and juggling.

The circus may have rejected them but Art had not, that was what Herr Blomgren said. They still served Art, and Art deserved their loyalty unto death! Artistes! Artistes forever! That was Herr Blomgren's opinion and Fru Blomgren shared it.

Hede walked in silence, listening to him. His thoughts jumped restlessly from one idea to another. There are times when one encounters things that stand out as symbols, as signs to be interpreted. There was some meaning in what was happening to him just now. If he could come to a true understanding of it, it would offer him guidance in reaching a wise decision.

Herr Blomgren asked the student to look a little more

carefully at the girl leading the blind man. Had he ever seen such eyes? Did he not think that eyes like that must mean something? Was it possible to have eyes like that without being destined for something great?

Hede turned round and looked at the pale little girl. Yes indeed, her eyes shone like stars in her sad, rather gaunt face.

'Our Lord always knows what He is doing,' Fru Blomgren said, 'and I do believe He has some purpose in letting an artiste like Herr Blomgren perform on the street. But what was His purpose when He gave the girl those eyes and that smile?'

'Let me tell you something,' Herr Blomgren said. 'She does not have the slightest aptitude for Art. And with those eyes!'

Hede was beginning to suspect that they were not actually talking to him but giving a lecture to the girl, who was walking right behind them and could hear every word.

'She's no older than thirteen, which is certainly not too old to learn things, but impossible, just impossible since she has no aptitude. Teach her to sew, sir, if you don't want to waste your time. But don't teach her to stand on her head!'

'That smile of hers makes people quite mad about her,' Herr Blomgren said. 'That smile alone means that she is constantly receiving offers from families wanting to adopt her. She could be growing up in a well-to-do household by now if only she would give up her grandfather. But what is the point of a smile which drives people crazy if she is never going to perform on horseback or the trapeze?'

'We know other artistes,' Fru Blomgren said, 'who take children from the street and train them ready to take over when they themselves are no longer capable of performing. There are some people who have managed to create stars and make people pay enormous sums to see them perform. But Herr Blomgren and I have never thought of the money, we have just imagined what it would be like to see Ingrid flying through a hoop while the whole circus shook with the applause. For us that would have been like starting life anew.'

'Why do we retain her grandfather?' Herr Blomgren asked. 'Is he an artiste who brings us any credit? We, being who we are, we could have taken on a retired member of the royal orchestra, you know. But we love the girl, we can't do without her, and we keep the old man on for her sake.'

'It's cruel of her, isn't it, not to allow us to turn her into an artiste?' they said.

Hede looked around. The little girl, the blind man's guide, was walking along, her face set in a look of patient suffering. He could see that she understood that anyone who could not perform on the tightrope was a talentless creature, worthy only of contempt.

By that point they had just arrived at another courtyard and before they began their performance Hede sat down on an upturned wheelbarrow and began preaching.

He set about defending the poor girl who was guiding the blind man. He reproached Herr and Fru Blomgren for wanting to deliver her up to the great and cruel public, a public that would love her and applaud her for a while but which – the moment she was old and worn out – would abandon her, leaving her to trudge the streets in the rain and cold of autumn. No, someone who could make just one person happy was already an artiste. The girl, Ingrid, should keep her eyes and smile for just one person, she should save them for that person alone – and that person would not desert her but provide her with a sheltered home as long as he lived.

Hede's eyes filled with tears as he said this. He was talking to himself more than to the others. He suddenly felt how terrible it was to be driven out into the world, to be separated from a quiet home life.

And now he saw the girl's great starry eyes begin to shine. It was as though she had understood every word. It was as though she once more dared to live.

But Herr Blomgren and his wife grew very earnest. They pressed Hede's hand and promised that they would never again try to push the girl into becoming an artiste. She could follow whatever path she chose. He had moved them. They were artistes, passionate artistes, and they understood what he meant when he spoke of loyalty and love.

After that Hede parted from them and went home. He made no further attempt to draw some hidden meaning from his adventure. When all was said and done, the only point of it all had been to save that poor sorrowing child from pining away over her own inadequacy.

II

Munkhyttan, Gunnar Hede's estate and manor house, lay far away in a poor forest parish in the west of Dalarna. And a big and desolate parish it was, a harsh and barren landscape on all sides. Most of the area consisted of rocky tree-covered hills and small lochans. People would not have been able to make a living there had they not had the right to range far and wide as pedlars. As a result of that, however, this poor district was full of old tales of penniless peasant boys and peasant girls who had set out with a sack of knick-knacks on their backs only to return home riding in a golden coach with coffers full of money.

One of the very best of these tales told of Hede's grandfather. He had been the son of an impecunious fiddler, had grown up with the fiddle and at the age of seventeen set out with his sack of wares. And wherever he went he used the fiddle to help him sell his wares, sometimes playing for people to come and dance whilst also selling them silk scarves and combs and needles. His trading was always accompanied by much laughter and fun and things went so well that he was eventually able to purchase Munkhyttan with its iron mine and foundry from its destitute owner.

And so he became a laird and married the beautiful daughter of the old proprietor.

From then on they were always referred to as the old gentlefolk and the only thing they thought about was beautifying and improving their property. They were the ones who moved the manor house out onto a pretty island close to the shore of the small lake around which their fields and mine workings lay. The upper floor was added during their time because they liked having the space to entertain a lot of people, and they also added the grand external double staircase. They planted the whole of the island with broad-leaved trees, constructed narrow winding paths through the rocky ground and built small belvederes that hung out over the lake like big bird's nests. They were the ones who imported the Dutch furniture and the Italian violin and the French roses that lined the terrace; it was they who had a wall built to protect the orchard from the north wind, and they were the ones who started the vinery.

The old gentlefolk had been happy and friendly old-fashioned people. It's true that the lady liked putting on airs just a little, but not the old gentleman. In spite of all the splendour in which he lived he was keen to remember what he once had been, and in the office where he did his work and where everyone came to see him, his pedlar's sack and his red-painted home-made fiddle hung above the old man's desk.

The sack and the fiddle remained hanging there even after his death, and every time the old man's son and grandson saw them they were filled with gratitude. Those humble tools were what had created Munkhyttan and Munkhyttan was the best thing in the world.

Whatever the reason may have been – and no doubt it was mainly because this was the sort of home where a good, kindly and carefree life seemed natural – the Hedes clung to the place with more love than was good for them. Gunnar Hede in particular was so attached to the property that people said of him that it was quite wrong to say he owned an estate: the contrary was true – there was an old place in the west of Dalarna that owned Gunnar Hede.

If he had not turned himself into a slave to this huge draughty old manor house with a few acres of arable land and forest, along with some deformed apple trees, Hede would probably have continued his studies or, better still, set about studying music, which undoubtedly seemed to be his true vocation in the world. But when he came home from Uppsala and took stock of the situation only to find that the estate really would have to be sold unless he could earn a great deal of money rather quickly, he threw all his other plans overboard and decided to set out as a pedlar just as his grandfather had done.

Hede's mother and his fiancée begged him to sell the estate rather than sacrifice himself for it, but he was not to be moved. He dressed in peasant clothing, bought a stock of goods and began roaming the country as a pedlar. He believed that with just a couple of years' trading he would be able to earn enough to pay the debts and save the estate.

And as far as the estate was concerned, his enterprise was successful. But he brought dreadful misfortune down upon himself.

After travelling with his pack of wares for about a year it occurred to him to try to make a large sum of money all at once. So he went up to the far north of the country and bought goats, many goats, it must have been a couple of hundred. He and a friend were planning to drive all these animals down to a market in Värmland, where goats cost twice as much as up in the north. If he could sell all his goats he would be pulling off a wonderful piece of business.

It was only November and as yet there was no snow on the ground when Hede and his companion set off with their large herd of goats. Everything went well the first day, but on the second day, when they were in the great Seventy-Mile Forest, it began to snow. There was a heavy fall of snow accompanied by a strong wind and spindrift. The animals soon found it difficult to make any progress through the snow. Goats are without doubt both brave and hardy beasts and they struggled on for a long time, but the whirling snow lasted for several days and nights and the cold was dreadful.

Hede did everything he could to save the animals, but once the snow began to fall he was unable to get either fodder or water for them. And after a day's tramping through deep snow the skin on their legs was torn and they were in such pain that they did not want to go any farther. Hede picked up the first goat that threw itself down at the roadside and refused to rise and follow the herd and he carried it on his shoulders. But when another lay down, and then a third, he could not carry them all. There was nothing he could do but look the other way and walk on.

You have perhaps heard of the Seventy-Mile Forest? Not a farm, not a cabin for mile after mile, just forest. Tall pine trees with hard bark and branches high up, not young trees with tender bark and tender twigs that the animals can eat. But for the snow they could have passed through the forest in a matter of days, but now they could not get through at all. All the goats remained there and the men came close to perishing too.

They met no one along the whole path. No one helped them.

Hede tried to dig the snow away so the goats could eat moss, but the snow just went on falling and falling and the moss was frozen hard to the ground. And how could he possibly find fodder for two hundred animals anyway?

He bore it bravely until the goats began to bleat pitifully. They had been a jolly, high-spirited and quite unruly crowd on the first day and he'd had his work cut out making sure they all stayed with the herd and did not butt each other to death. But now they seemed to realise there was nothing they could do to save themselves and they changed character, losing all their courage. They all began to bleat and wail, not weakly and faintly as goats usually do, but very noisily and louder and louder as their distress grew. And when he heard this bleating he began to think he would go mad.

The forest was wild and desolate and there was no hope of help. One animal after another sank by the wayside. The snow whirled around them and covered them, and when Hede looked back along this line of snowdrifts, each marking the corpse of an animal with only the horns and hooves showing, his brain began to reel.

He rushed at the animals that were letting the snow drift over them, swung his switch at them and struck them. It was the only way to save them, after all, but still they would not move. He grabbed them by the horns and dragged them onwards and they let themselves be dragged, but they did not take a single step for themselves. When he let go of their horns they licked his hands as if begging him to help. As soon as he approached them they licked his hands.

All this had such an appalling effect on Hede that he felt he was going mad.

It is impossible to be certain, however, whether things would have turned out so badly for him after that dreadful business in the forest if he had not gone to visit someone he loved dearly. Not his mother, but his fiancée. He convinced himself that he must go to her at once and tell her he had lost so much money that it would be impossible for him to marry for many years. But there can be little doubt that his real reason for going to her was simply because he wanted to hear her say that she loved him as much as before despite his misfortune. He believed she would be able to drive away the memory of the Seventy-Mile Forest.

And perhaps she could have done, but she chose not to. She had been displeased from the moment he began going around with his pedlar's pack and looking like a peasant. And for that reason she felt it was difficult to love him as she had loved him before. When she now heard that he would be doing this for many years to come, she said that she could no longer wait for him. And that is when Hede almost lost his mind.

He did not go completely mad and he retained enough sanity to carry on his trade. In fact he did even better business than other pedlars and was always welcome among the peasants because people enjoyed making fun of him. People teased him mercilessly but, in a sense, that was all to the good because what he really wanted was to get rich.

After just a few years he had indeed earned enough to pay off all the debts and to live a carefree life on his estate. But by then he was incapable of understanding that fact and so he continued instead going from farm to farm in the same mad, half-witted way, no longer conscious of being a gentleman.

III

Råglanda was the name of a remote parish in eastern Värmland, very close to the border with Dalarna. There was a large deanery there, but the manse in which the minister lived was a poor little place. But poor as they were in that little manse, the minister and his wife had been kind enough to take in a foster child. She was a girl called Ingrid and she had come to the house when she was thirteen years old.

The minister had been at market and chanced to see her sitting weeping outside a circus tent. He stopped and asked her why she was crying and he learnt that her blind grandfather had died and she no longer had any near relatives. She was travelling with a pair of acrobats, who had been kind to her, but she was upset now because she was too stupid to learn how to dance on the tightrope and thus help earn money.

There was something so sweet about the child's grief that the minister was moved and fascinated. Without hesitation he told himself that he could not leave such a little creature to lead a squalid life among homeless itinerants. He went to the acrobats' tent, where he met Herr and Fru Blomgren, and he offered to take the child into his home. The old artistes had begun to weep, saying that although the girl was quite incapable of working as an artiste they would have liked to keep her. But they thought she might be happier in a real home with people who lived in the same place all year round. For that reason they would let the minister take her, but only on condition that he promised she would be treated like one of his own children.

He gave them his word and the girl had lived at the manse

ever since. She was a quiet gentle child who showed affection and tenderness to all around her. At first her foster-parents loved her dearly, but as she grew older she developed a marked tendency to drift off into dreams and fantasies. The realm of visions and imagination exerted such a strong attraction that she would abandon her work and lose herself in dreams in the middle of the day. The minister's wife, a brisk and stern hard-working woman, had no time for this. She complained that the girl was lazy and slothful and she treated her so harshly that the girl became frightened and unhappy.

When she was nineteen years old the girl fell seriously ill. No one really knew what the matter was because all this took place so long ago that there was no doctor in Råglanda. But things looked bad for the girl. Everyone could see that she was so ill that she seemed certain to die.

She herself did nothing but pray to Our Lord to allow her to depart this life. She wanted so much to die, she said.

It really seemed as if Our Lord was intent on testing how serious she was, for one night she felt her whole body grow stiff and cold and a profound torpor came upon her.

'This must surely be death,' she said to herself.

But the strange thing was that she did not lose consciousness completely. She knew she was lying there as if dead, knew they were wrapping her in a shroud and laying her in a coffin, but she felt neither anxiety nor fear about being buried alive. She had only one thought in her mind, which was that she was fortunate to be allowed to die and leave this cruel life.

The only thing that worried her was that they might discover she was not really dead and would not bury her. How bitter her life must have been for her to be so entirely unafraid of death.

But not a single person noticed she was alive. She was driven to the church, carried into the churchyard and lowered into her grave.

As is the custom in Råglanda her funeral took place before the Sunday morning service, but the grave was not filled immediately. The mourners had gone into the church leaving the coffin in the open grave and they were intending to come and help the gravedigger to fill it in as soon as the service was over.

The girl knew everything that was going on but felt no fear. Even had she wanted to she would have been quite unable to make a movement to show she was alive, and even had she been capable of moving she would have stayed still. She really was happy to be close to death.

To say that she was alive would not really have been true anyway. She was not in possession of her senses nor was she conscious in any normal way. The only part of her that was still alive was that part of the soul that dreams at night.

She was even beyond thinking how dreadful it would be if she woke after her grave had been filled in. She had no more control of her mind than a dreamer has.

'I wonder,' she thought, 'whether there is anything in the whole wide world capable of giving me the will to live.'

No sooner had she had this thought than it seemed as if the lid of her coffin and the cloth over her face became transparent and she saw before her pretty clothes and money and beautiful gardens with lovely fruit.

'No, I don't care about any of that,' she said, closing her eyes to all the splendours.

When she looked up again they had all gone, but there instead of them, quite clearly and distinctly, she saw a little angel of the Lord sitting on the edge of the grave.

'Good morning, little angel of God!' she said to him.

'Good morning, Ingrid!' the angel said. 'While you are lying here with nothing to do, I shall tell you about the olden times.'

Ingrid could hear quite clearly every word the angel said, but his voice was unlike anything she had heard before. It sounded most like a stringed instrument whose notes were words, but it did not resemble song, being more like the music of a fiddle or a harp.

'Ingrid,' the angel said, 'do you remember that when your grandfather was still alive you met a young student who walked with you from one courtyard to another for a whole day and played your grandfather's fiddle?'

The girl appeared to be dead but her face lit up in a smile.

'Do you think I have forgotten that?' she said. 'Not a day has passed since then without me thinking of him.'

'And not a night without you dreaming about him?'

'No, not a night without me dreaming about him.'

'And you still want to die even though you remember him so well?' the angel said. 'Which means, of course, you will never be able to see him again.'

When he said this the girl seemed to understand all the beauty of love, but not even that could tempt her.

'No, no,' she said, 'I am afraid to live. I would rather die.'

Then the angel waved his hand and Ingrid saw before her a great barren desert of sand. It was treeless and bare, dry and hot, and it stretched on and on endlessly. Here and there there were things lying on the sand. At first glance they looked like scattered rocks but when she looked more closely she saw they were animals, enormous living monsters with powerful claws and great gaping jaws full of teeth. And they lay there on the sand waiting for prey. And between these terrible beasts the student was walking, walking unconcernedly and with no suspicion that the shapes around him were alive.

'But warn him, warn him!' Ingrid said to the angel, filled with unspeakable anxiety. 'Tell him they're alive, tell him he must take care!'

'I am not allowed to speak to him,' the angel said in his ringing voice. 'You must warn him yourself!'

The girl who seemed to be dead realised with horror that she was lying powerless and incapable of hurrying to save the student. She made one vain effort after another to rise but she was powerless, locked as she was in the embrace of death. And then, and then! She felt how her heart began to beat, how the blood began to surge through her veins, how the stiffness of death left her body. She rose and hastened towards him – – – –

IV

There is nothing so certain as the fact that the sun loves the open spaces in front of small country churches. Hasn't anyone ever noticed that there is more sunshine to be seen outside a little whitewashed church during the morning service than is ever seen elsewhere? Nowhere else do the sunbeams weave such a tight web of light, nowhere else does the air remain so solemnly still. The sun stands guard, ensuring that the congregation does not stay outside the church gossiping. It wants them all to go in and sit quietly listening to the sermon. That is why it sends down such a wealth of rays outside the walls of a church.

It is perhaps impossible to be quite certain that the sun keeps watch outside small churches every single Sunday, but what is certain is that on the morning the girl who seemed to be dead had been laid in her grave in the churchyard at Råglanda a fierce heat spread across the small open space in front of the church. Even the small pebbles lying glittering in the ruts left by cartwheels looked as if they might catch fire. The short trampled grass curled up until it resembled dry moss, while the yellow dandelions that adorned the grass puffed themselves up on their long stalks until they were as big as asters.

A man from Dalarna came walking down the road – one of those pedlars who go round the country selling knives and scissors. He was wearing a long white sheepskin coat and he had a big black leather pack on his back. He had been walking for several hours carrying all that and had not felt the heat, but when he left the highway and entered the space outside the church he had not been there more than a minute before having to stop and take his hat off to wipe the sweat from his brow.

Standing there with his head bared he looked both handsome and intelligent. His brow was high and white, the deep furrow between his eyebrows was suggestive of much thought, his mouth was well-formed and his lips thin. His hair was parted in the middle, slightly curly at the ends and shaped around the nape of his neck but still covering his ears. He was tall and strongly built without being coarse – well-proportioned, in fact, in every way. But he had one defect, which was that his gaze was unsteady, the pupils constantly shifting right into the corners of his eyes as if trying to hide away. And there were twisted lines around his mouth that hinted at madness, at something foolish and slack, at something that did not fit, did not really go with the face.

And he could not have been completely right in the head because here he was traipsing around with his heavy pack on a Sunday. If he had been in full possession of his senses he would have known it was unnecessary since he could not sell anything anyway. None of the other Dalarna pedlars who worked the district would bend their backs under a pack on a Sunday, instead they would enter the Lord's house as upright and unburdened as everyone else.

No doubt this poor fellow did not know it was the Sabbath until he stopped in the sunshine outside the church and heard the singing of hymns. But then he had enough sense left to know that he could not carry on his trade that day and his mind was faced with the dreadful task of wondering where to spend his free day.

For a long time he simply stood and stared straight ahead. When everything was proceeding as usual he had no difficulty managing. He was not so far gone that he was incapable of filling the weekdays going from farm to farm plying his trade. But he could never get used to Sundays. They always crept up on him as a great and unforeseen problem.

His eyes suddenly became fixed and the muscles in his forehead swelled.

The first thought that entered his mind was probably to

go into the church and listen to the singing. But he rejected that idea. He really did want to hear the singing but he did not dare go into the church. It was not the people he was afraid of, but in some churches there were strange and frightening pictures depicting creatures he would rather not think about.

At last his mind worked its way to the thought that since this was a church there must surely be a churchyard. And if he had a churchyard to go to his troubles were over. It would have been impossible to offer him anything better. Whenever he saw a churchyard from a road he was travelling along, he would turn aside and sit there for a while even if it was the middle of the working week.

But now that he wanted to go to the churchyard a new difficulty suddenly arose. The trouble was that the burial ground in Råglanda is not right beside the church, which stands on a rocky hillock, but in a small meadow beyond the parish hall. And it was impossible for him to reach the churchyard gate without passing along a road on which the church-goers' horses were tethered.

All the horses were standing with their heads bent into bundles of hay or bags of oats, chewing so loudly that their teeth could be heard crunching the fodder. There was no question they would do him any harm, but he had his own ideas about the perils of walking past a long line of animals like this one.

He made two or three attempts but his courage failed him and he had to turn back. He was not afraid that the horses would bite or kick him, it was quite enough that they were close enough to look at him. It was quite enough that they could rattle their halter-chains or scrape the ground with their hooves.

At last there came a moment when all the horses were looking down and seemed to be trying to outdo one another at eating. That was when he began walking between them. He gathered his sheepskin coat tightly around him so it would not flap and give him away and he walked on tiptoe as neatly as he could. If a horse raised its eyes and looked at him, he stopped at once and gave a kind of bob or curtsey. In a situation as dangerous as this he really wanted to be well-mannered, and surely the animals would be sensible enough to understand that he could not bow when he had a sack of iron goods on his back. The only thing he could do was bob.

He sighed deeply, for it is a hard and troublesome thing in this life to be afraid – as he was – of all four-legged animals. As a matter of fact he was not really afraid of anything but goats and he would not have been in the least afraid of horses and dogs and cats if only he could have been certain that they were not some kind of transformed goat. But he could never be sure of that, which meant that his situation was just as bad as if he had been afraid of all four-legged creatures.

Reminding himself how strong he was and that these little farm horses were usually quite harmless was of no help. A man with fear lodged in his soul does not think like that. It is a dreadful thing, fear, and a heavy burden for those in whom it dwells.

But, remarkably enough, he did get past the whole row of horses. He did the last bit in two long jumps and once inside the churchyard he closed the iron gate behind him and stood there shaking his fist at the horses.

'You worthless, you wretched, you accursed billy-goats!'

He did that to all animals, unable to stop himself calling them billy-goats. And this was very foolish of him because it had earned him a name he did not want: everyone he met called him Billy Goat. He had no desire to be addressed in that way and wanted people to call him by his proper name, but no one in this part of the country seemed to know what that name was.

He stood by the gate for a while, relishing his escape from the horses, but he soon walked farther into the churchyard. He stopped and gave a bob at every cross and stone, but now it had nothing to do with fear, now it was just because he was pleased to see these dear old acquaintances. His expression became gentle and pleasant. He had met the same crosses and the same stones so often before! Just the same as ever! How well he knew them! He must say Good Morning to them.

He was so fond of churchyards. They did not usually have

animals grazing in them and there were no people to make fun of him. It was best when they were deserted, as this one was now, but even when there were people present they did not usually disturb him. Of course he knew many beautiful meadows and pastures that could be even more pleasing, but people never left him in peace in places like that. They simply could not be compared with churchyards. Churchyards were even better than the forest itself, for the solitude in the forest was so desolate that it frightened him. Here it was as still as in the depths of the forest, but here he had company, here there were people sleeping under every stone and every mound. Just enough company for him not to feel lonely and ill at ease.

He made his way at once towards the newly dug grave. He went there partly because it lay in the shade of some trees and partly because he liked company. He no doubt thought that someone interred so recently would be better protection against loneliness than those who had passed away long before.

With his back to the big mound of sandy soil at the side of the grave he bent his knees and managed to push his pack up so that it rested firmly on the mound, and then he undid the coarse leather straps that fastened it to him. It was a great day, a holiday, and he even took off his sheepskin coat. With a feeling of great contentment he sat on the grass so close to the grave that his long legs in their knee-length stockings and heavy laced boots hung down over the edge.

He made himself sit still for quite a long time, eyes fixed on the coffin. When you bear within you as much fear as he did, it is impossible to be careful enough. But the coffin did not move at all and there was no reason to suspect that anything was lurking there.

As soon as he was certain of that he put his hand into the side pocket of his pack and took out a fiddle and bow. At the same time he nodded to the body in the grave which, since it was lying so still, was about to be allowed to hear something very lovely.

This was a very rare thing indeed, as few people were permitted to hear him play. The people on the farms where they set the dogs on him and called him Billy Goat were never allowed to hear him. But it was not unknown for him to play in a cottage where the people talked in low voices and moved quietly and did not ask him whether he wanted to buy goatskins. In a place like that he would take out his fiddle and play. And it was a great mark of favour, the greatest he could show anyone.

Now, as he sat there on the edge of the grave and played, it did not sound at all bad. He did not play a wrong note and he played so gently and softly that it would scarcely have been audible over by the next grave.

The truly amazing thing was that it wasn't actually the man from Dalarna who could play, it was the fiddle itself that remembered a few little tunes. They emerged as soon as he stroked the fiddle with the bow. It would not perhaps have meant a great deal to anyone else, but to him, a man unable to remember a single tune for himself, the possession of a fiddle that could play itself was the most precious gift of all.

As he played he sat beaming and smiling like someone listening to the babbling and chattering of a child. It was the fiddle that talked and talked and he just listened. But it was so strange that sounds of such beauty could be heard as soon as he passed the bow across the strings: the fiddle took care of it all, knew how it should go, and the man from Dalarna – well, he just sat and listened.

Tunes grew out of that fiddle as grass grows from the earth. No one could understand how it happened. It was simply something ordained by Our Lord.

The man from Dalarna had been intending to stay the whole day, allowing the sweet tones to grow from the fiddle like small flowers, white and many-coloured. He was going to play until he had a whole meadow full of flowers, play until the whole long valley was filled and the whole wide plain.

But the girl who was lying apparently dead in her coffin – she must have heard the fiddle playing and the effect it had on her was wondrous. The tones made her dream and she was so stirred by what she saw in her dream that her heart began to beat and her blood to circulate. And she woke.

Now it is important to understand that everything she had experienced while lying apparently dead, all the thoughts she had had and even that last dream, all that was gone and forgotten the moment she woke to normal consciousness. She did not even know that she was lying in her coffin, she thought she was still lying ill in her bed at home. She did think it strange that she was still alive. Just now, before falling asleep, she had been gasping in her death throes and it should all have ended some time ago. She had bid farewell to her foster-parents, her brothers and sisters and the servants. The dean himself had come and given her Holy Communion because her foster-father could not bear to do it. She had turned her thoughts away from earthly things many days before. It was strange that she was not dead.

She was surprised at how dark it was in the room in which she lay since there had always been a lighted candle burning every night since she became ill. And they had let the covers slip off her, too, so she was lying there cold as ice.

She raised herself up a little in order to pull the covers over her. And she struck her head against the lid of the coffin and fell back with a little cry of pain.

The blow to her head had been quite hard and she immediately lost consciousness again. She lay there motionless as before and it seemed that all life had left her once more. The man from Dalarna, who had heard both the blow and the cry, put down his fiddle at once and began to listen. But nothing more was heard, nothing at all.

He began watching the coffin as closely as when he had first arrived. He sat nodding, as if agreeing with an unspoken thought, which was that there is nothing on this earth that can be depended on. Here he thought he had found the very best and quietest of friends, but was this friend going to let him down too?

He sat looking at the coffin as if trying to see right through it. At last, when the silence remained unbroken, he picked up the fiddle again and began to play.

But now the fiddle refused. However gently and caressingly he stroked it, it would no longer produce a melody. It was so sad that he came close to tears. He had been meaning to sit quietly and listen to his fiddle all day, but now it would not play.

He thought he knew the reason. The fiddle was uneasy and afraid of whatever it was that had moved down in the grave. It had forgotten all its tunes and could think of nothing apart from what might have been knocking on the lid of the coffin. That's the way of things, after all: when you are afraid, you forget everything.

He realised he would have to calm the fiddle if he wanted to hear more.

Everything had been going so well, better than for years. If there really was something dangerous in the coffin would it not be best to let it out? That would satisfy the fiddle and the beautiful flowers would once again begin to grow from it.

Full of resolve he opened his big pack and began rummaging through knives, saws and axe-heads until he found a screwdriver. A moment later he was down in the grave on his hands and knees unscrewing the lid of the coffin.

He took out screw after screw until at last he was able to lift the lid and lean it against the side of the grave. And at that moment the cloth slipped off the face of the seemingly lifeless girl.

As soon as the fresh air reached her Ingrid opened her eyes. And now she saw light all around her: they must have moved her for now she was lying in a yellow room with a green ceiling which had a large chandelier hanging from it.

The room was narrow and the bed very narrow indeed. Why did it feel as if her arms and legs had been tied? Was it to hold her still in this tiny, tiny bed?

And it was strange that they had put a hymn-book under her chin. Surely that was only done with corpses?

She was holding a small bouquet of flowers in her fingers. Her foster-mother had cut a few sprigs of flowering myrtle and put them in her hands. Ingrid was surprised: what could possibly have come over her foster-mother?

She saw that they had given her a neatly pleated cambric sheet and a pillow with a wide lace border. She was pleased.

She liked nice things around her. But she would have preferred a warm quilt: it surely couldn't be good for someone who was ill to be lying uncovered?

Ingrid was so bitterly cold she was on the point of putting her hands over her eyes and weeping.

At that moment, however, she felt something cool and hard against her cheek and she began to smile. The old red wooden horse, three-legged Camilla, was lying beside her on the pillow. Her little brother, who could not go a single night without the horse beside him in his bed, had put it in with her. That was such a loving thing to do. Ingrid felt even closer to tears when she thought of her little brother trying to comfort her with his wooden horse.

But she did not come to tears, for the truth suddenly dawned on her. Little brother had given her his wooden horse and mother had given her the white myrtle flowers and they had placed the hymn-book under her chin because they all thought she was dead.

Ingrid took hold of the edge of the coffin with both hands and sat up. The narrow little bed was a coffin and the yellow room was a grave. It was so difficult to understand. She simply could not comprehend that this involved her, that she had been shrouded and placed in a grave. She must be lying at home in her own bed imagining or dreaming these things, mustn't she? Surely it would soon become clear that none of this was true and everything would return to normal?

The explanation suddenly came to her. 'I often have strange dreams,' she thought. 'This must just be a vision I'm having.' She heaved a sigh of satisfaction and lay back in the coffin, now utterly certain that this was her own old bed, which – like this one – wasn't very wide.

While all this was going on the man from Dalarna was standing in the grave by Ingrid's feet. He was standing no more than a few feet from her but she had not seen him. It wasn't only because he had tried to crouch in a corner and make himself invisible as soon as the dead girl in the coffin opened her eyes and began to move. She would probably have noticed him even though he was holding the coffin lid in front of him like a shield if it had not been for a kind of white mist that hung before her eyes. She was only able to see things clearly when they were very close. Ingrid was not even able to see that she was surrounded by walls of sand, that she had taken the sun to be a great chandelier and the vault of linden leaves to be the ceiling.

The poor fellow from Dalarna stood waiting for whatever it was that was moving in the coffin to go away. He simply assumed it would go of its own accord – after all, it had knocked because it wanted to get out. He stood for a long time with his head behind the coffin lid expecting it to go. He peeped out when he thought it must have departed, but it had not moved. It was still lying there on a bed of wood shavings.

This did not please him. He wanted a quick conclusion. It was a long time since his fiddle had spoken as beautifully as it had spoken today and he was longing to be sitting peacefully with it again.

Ingrid, who had almost fallen asleep, suddenly heard herself being addressed in the sing-song speech of Dalarna.

'It must be about time for you to get up, I think.'

As soon as he said this he hid his head. He was trembling so much at his own boldness that he almost dropped the lid of the coffin.

The white mist clouding Ingrid's eyes vanished completely on hearing a human voice. She saw a man squeezed in the corner at the end of the grave and he was holding a coffin lid in front of him. She realised instantly that she could not just lie down and dismiss this as a dream vision. This was something real and she needed to sort it out for herself. There seemed to be no question that the coffin was a coffin and the grave a grave and that just a few minutes earlier she, Ingrid, had been no more than a corpse, both shrouded and interred.

For the first time she felt horrified by what had happened to her. Lord, just think about it! She really could have been dead by now! She could have been a foul decaying corpse. She had been lowered into her grave, waiting for sand and earth to be shovelled down on her; she had been no more than an insignificant clod of turf; she had been utterly cast aside. Worms would have been welcome to eat her and no one would have been in the least concerned.

In the terrifying state in which Ingrid found herself she felt such a need to have a human being at her side. She had immediately recognised Billy Goat when he had poked his head out a moment ago. He had been a familiar face at the manse and she was not at all afraid of him. She wanted him to come close to her now. She did not mind in the least that he was mad. He was a human being – a living human being. She wanted him to come close enough for her to feel that she belonged among the living and not among the dead.

'Oh, for God's sake come to me!' she said in a voice close to tears. She sat up in the coffin and held out her arms to him.

But the man from Dalarna still had his wits about him. When she wanted to coax him to come to her he decided to set his own conditions.

'I'll come as long as you will go away,' he said.

Ingrid immediately attempted to obey him and get out of the coffin, but she was so tightly wrapped in the sheet that she was unable to stand up.

'You'll have to come and help me,' she said, half from fear and half because her joints were numb. And she felt such a need to be close to a living being.

He did come, pushing his way through between the coffin and the side of the grave. He bent over her, lifted her out of the grave and set her down on the green grass at the graveside.

Ingrid could not stop herself throwing both arms around his neck, laying her head on his shoulder and sobbing. Afterwards she found it hard to understand how she had been able to bring herself to do so, why she had not been frightened of him. It was partly joy that he was a human being, a living human being, and partly gratitude that he had saved her.

Good God, what would have become of her had it not been for him! He was the one who had lifted the lid of the coffin and brought her back to life. She did not know, of course, how any of it had happened, but there was no doubt he was the one who had opened the coffin. What would have become of her if he had not done so? She would have woken imprisoned in the black coffin. She would have knocked and shouted. Who would have heard her when she was six feet beneath the earth? Ingrid did not dare think about it, she was simply overcome with gratitude at being saved. She had to have someone to thank. She had to have someone's shoulder on which to rest her head as she wept in gratitude.

Perhaps the most remarkable thing to happen that day was that the man from Dalarna did not push her away. But he was not absolutely certain that she was alive and he knew it was inadvisable to fail to obey a dead person. As soon as he could he freed himself from her arms and went down into the grave. He placed the lid back on the coffin, put in the screws and fastened it properly just as it had been before. Surely now the coffin would remain still and his fiddle would once again feel at peace and regain its melodies.

During this time Ingrid was sitting on the grass trying to gather her thoughts. She looked over towards the church and saw horses and carriages and began to understand the situation. It was Sunday and they had laid her in her grave in the morning and were now in the church.

She was seized by great terror. The service would soon be over and people would come out and catch sight of her. And here she was, wearing nothing but a sheet – to all intents and purposes naked. Heaven preserve her from so many people seeing her in that state! They would never forget it. She would have to live with the shame for the rest of her life.

She wondered where she could get clothes. She thought for a moment of quickly putting on the man's sheepskin coat, but she did not think that was likely to make her look more like an ordinary human being.

She turned quickly to the mad fellow, who was still working on the lid of the coffin.

'Listen to me,' she said. 'You must let me crawl into your pack.'

In a flash she was over by his leather pack, which was big enough to carry all the goods for a whole stall, and began to tear it open.

'Oh, please, please, come and help me!'

She did not ask in vain. As soon as the man saw her touching his bag he came up out of the grave at once.

'You there, what are you up to with my pack?' he said in a threatening way.

Still counting him as her best friend Ingrid paid no attention to his harsh tone.

'Oh please, oh please,' she said, 'help me so that the congregation doesn't come out and see me! Empty out your wares somewhere and let me get into the sack and then carry me home! Do it, do it please! I'm from the manse and it's only a little way away. You must know where it is.'

The man stood looking at her, his expression completely vacant. She could not tell whether he understood a word of what she had said.

She repeated it, but he showed no sign of obeying her.

She began hurling things out of his sack again and he stamped his foot at her and grabbed the sack.

God in Heaven, how was Ingrid to get him to obey her?

There was a fiddle and a bow lying on the grass beside her. She picked them up, she had no idea why. Probably because she had spent so much time with fiddlers that she could not bear to see an instrument lying on the ground.

As soon as she touched the fiddle he let go the sack, came over and snatched the instrument from her.

The fact she had touched his fiddle seemed to drive him crazy. He looked vicious.

What on earth could she come up with in order to escape before it was time for the congregation to emerge?

She began to promise him all sorts of wonderful things, just as you do with children when you want them to be good.

'I'll tell my father to buy at least a dozen scythes off you. I'll lock up all the dogs when you come to the manse. I'll ask mother to give you a really good meal.'

He showed no sign of giving way.

Then she thought of the fiddle and she said despairingly:

'If you'll carry me to the manse I'll play the fiddle for you.'

And behold, a smile spread across his face! That was undoubtedly what he wanted.

'I'll play the fiddle to you all afternoon, I'll play as long as you want.'

'Will you teach the fiddle new tunes?' he asked.

'I'll certainly do that!'

What followed, however, made Ingrid both surprised and downhearted. He took a firm hold of the bag and pulled it towards him. Then he dragged it away across the graves, flattening the penny-cress and southernwood growing on them as if it were a roller.

He took it as far as a heap of dried leaves, brushwood and old funeral bouquets that lay by the churchyard wall. There he pulled out everything he had in his pack and concealed it all carefully under the heap.

When it was empty he came back to Ingrid.

'Now you can get in!' he said.

Ingrid climbed into the pack and crouched down on its wooden bottom. The man tightened all the straps as carefully as if he were carrying his usual wares, bent down until he was almost on his knees, put his arms through the shoulder straps, adjusted a couple of belts that criss-crossed his chest and stood up. After walking a few steps he began to laugh. The pack he had on his back was so light he could have danced with it.

*

It was only a little over a mile from the church to the manse and the pedlar from Dalarna could cover a distance like that in twenty minutes. Ingrid's only desire was that he would go quickly enough to carry her home before the people in church and the funeral guests arrived. She simply could not bear being seen by so many people. The best thing would be for her to reach the house while only her foster-mother and the servant girls were there.

Ingrid had brought with her the small bunch of flowering myrtle placed in the coffin by her foster-mother. She was so pleased with it that she kissed it time after time. It made her think more kindly of her foster-mother than she had ever done before. But it was quite natural, of course, for the girl to be thinking kind thoughts about the woman: anyone returning straight from the grave will think kind and bright thoughts about everything that lives and moves upon the earth.

She had no difficulty in understanding that the minister's wife was bound to love the other children, her own children, much more than she could love her foster-daughter. And given that the family in the manse was so poor that they could not afford a nursemaid, she thought it perfectly natural that she should be the one to take care of her small brothers and sisters. If her brothers and sisters were unkind to her it was only because they were accustomed to her being their maid. It was not easy for them to remember that she had been taken into the family as a sister.

In the end, of course, it all came down to poverty. Were father ever to be appointed to a different living at some point, to become pastor or dean, everything would turn out well. Then it would be just as it had been in the early days when they all loved her. Oh, everything would surely go back to being as it used to be, wouldn't it? Ingrid kissed the flowers. Mother had probably not wanted to be unkind, it was poverty that had made her so unusually harsh.

Now, however, it no longer mattered to her how she was treated. Nothing could depress her from now on because she would always be happy to be alive. And if things should become difficult again she would only have to remember her little brother's Camilla and mother's myrtle flowers.

It was joy enough to know she was alive and being carried along the road. She would never have believed this morning that she would find herself travelling this winding and hilly road again. The smell of clover and the singing of the small birds and the shady beauty of the trees – all these had been things for the living to rejoice in, they had not been there for her.

But she did not have much time to think such thoughts as it only took the pedlar twenty minutes to reach the manse.

The minister's wife and the servant girls were at home alone, just as Ingrid had hoped. The minister's wife had been busy all morning preparing the funeral meal. Everything was now as good as ready and she was waiting for the guests to arrive. She had just been through to her bedroom to put on her black dress.

She looked out at the road to the church but there was still no sign of any carriages and so she took the opportunity to go back to the kitchen and taste the dishes.

She was glad that it had all turned out well – you can't help being pleased about that even when the house is in mourning. There was only one servant in the kitchen and since she was a girl who came from the minister's wife's home she felt she could speak to her in confidence.

'Well Lisa,' she said, 'I think anyone would be satisfied with a funeral feast like this.'

'I hope she can look down from above and see the show you are putting on for her,' Lisa said. 'She would be pleased.'

'Oh,' the minister's wife said, 'nothing that I do will ever please her.'

'She's dead now,' the servant girl said. 'It's not for me to say things about someone who's only just been buried.'

'I've often been on the receiving end of harsh words from my husband because of her,' the woman said.

The minister's wife was feeling the need to talk to someone about the dead girl. She was suffering pangs of conscience, which was why she had arranged such a grand funeral. She thought her conscience ought to have eased in view of all the trouble she had taken with the funeral but it had failed to do so. And her husband was suffering from his conscience too, saying that they had not treated the girl like one of their own children as they had promised when they adopted her. He said it would have been better if they had never taken her in since they had found it impossible to conceal the fact that they loved their own children more. So her foster-mother now felt the need to talk to someone in order to discover whether people thought she had been unkind to the girl.

She noticed that Lisa had begun to stir a pot very vigorously, as though having difficulty controlling her indignation. She was a canny girl who knew how to work her way into her mistress's good books.

'Anyone would think,' Lisa said, 'that if a girl has a mother who watches over her all the time and sees to it that she's clean and her clothes are mended, she'd be glad to obey her and try to please her. And when she's been given the chance to live in a good manse and be brought up above her station in life, you'd think she'd try to be useful and not just go round being stupid and dreaming. I have to ask myself what would have happened if the minister hadn't taken that poor girl in. She'd probably have just been a vagrant with those acrobats and eventually died as a slut on the street.'

It was just then that a man from Dalarna came walking across the yard, a fellow with a pack on his back even though it was a Sunday. He came in quietly through the open kitchen door, bobbing as he entered, though no one returned his greeting. Both the minister's wife and the servant girl saw him, but once they realised who it was they did not bother to interrupt their conversation.

The minister's wife was keen to continue. She realised she was about to hear exactly what she needed to ease her conscience.

'Perhaps it's just as well she's gone,' she said.

'I'll tell you what, ma'am,' the servant girl said eagerly, 'I do believe the Reverend thinks so too. Or he will soon enough. There'll be some peace in the house now, you see, and he'll be pleased about that.'

'Oh yes,' the minister's wife said, 'I had no choice but to go against him, did I? We were always having to spend money on clothes for her, indeed it became quite ridiculous. He was so anxious she should have as much as the others that she sometimes ended up with more. And once she was grown up she cost a lot.'

'I suppose you'll be letting Greta have her nettle-cloth dress now, ma'am?'

'Yes, either Greta will have it or I'll have it myself.'

'She's not leaving a great deal behind, poor soul.'

'No one was asking her to leave an inheritance,' her foster-mother said. 'I'd have been quite satisfied if we'd had a good word to remember her by.'

It was, of course, the kind of thing people say when their conscience is pricking them and they want to defend themselves. It bore not the slightest resemblance to what the minister's wife actually thought.

The pedlar from Dalarna behaved as he always did when he had come to sell his wares. He stood looking around the kitchen for a little while, then very slowly and deliberately propped his sack on a table and began undoing the various belts and straps. He looked all round once again to make sure that no cats or dogs were about to attack him, straightened his back and started to open the two leather flaps that were fastened with countless buckles and knots.

'There is no point in opening your pack today,' Lisa said. 'Today is Sunday and you must surely know that we don't buy things on Sundays?'

But she was not greatly bothered when the lunatic continued undoing the straps. Instead she turned back to the minister's wife, this being a good opportunity to curry favour.

'I don't know whether she was good to the children even. I often heard crying and wailing coming from the nursery.'

'She treated them like she treated their mother,' the minister's wife said. 'But now, of course, they're crying because she's dead.'

'They don't know what's good for them, ma'am,' the servant girl said. 'One thing you can be sure of, though, is that within a month no one will be weeping for her any longer.'

At that moment the two of them turned round from the stove and looked over to the table where the man was opening his large pack. They had heard something unexpected, something like a sigh or a sob. The man was just opening the inner flap when out of his sack emerged the foster-daughter they had buried, looking exactly as she had done when they placed her in her coffin.

She did not, in fact, look exactly as before. She was, so to speak, far less alive now than when they had laid her in her grave: her colour then had been almost as in life, but now her face was ghostly grey, her lips blue-black and her eyes dreadfully hollow and sunken.

She said nothing, but utter despair could be read in her face and, in a gesture of reproachful appeal, she held out to her foster-mother the bunch of myrtle flowers she had given her.

It was a sight beyond human endurance. Her foster-mother fell into a faint, the servant girl stood still for a moment looking at mother and daughter and then, covering her eyes with her hands, ran into her bed-closet and locked herself in.

'No, no,' she said, 'it's not me she has come for. I don't have to be part of this.'

But Ingrid turned to the pedlar.

'Shut me in again and carry me away from here! Do you hear me! Do you hear me! Carry me away from here! Carry me back to where you found me!'

At that moment the pedlar from Dalarna happened to look outside. A long row of carriages and carts were coming up the drive and into the yard. Oh no, oh no, he could not stay here! This was not for him!

Ingrid crouched at the bottom of his pack no longer caring about anything, just sobbing. The flaps and lids closed over her and she was lifted again onto the pedlar's back and carried away. The people arriving for the funeral feast laughed heartily at Billy Goat as he scuttled away, bobbing to one horse after another as he met them.

V

Old Anna Stina was a woman who lived deep in the forest. She used to help at the manse, coming down the hill as though in response to an unspoken call when there was baking or washing to be done. She was a kind and wise old soul and she and Ingrid were good friends. As soon as the girl was able to gather her thoughts, she decided to seek help from Anna Stina.

'Listen to me now,' she said to the pedlar. 'When you come to the high road you are to turn off into the forest. Go straight on until you come to a gate. That's where you turn left. Then go straight on again until you come to the big sandpit. You can see a cottage from there and that is where you are to take me. And that is where I shall play for you.'

The harsh and abrupt tone she adopted when giving him orders grated on her own ears. She had to speak like that in order to be obeyed, it was the only way. But who was she to be giving orders to anyone, anyway, when she didn't even have the right to live herself!

After this she would never be able to feel she had the right to live. That was the awful part of what had happened to her. She had been at the manse for six years and had not even managed to make them like her enough to want her to live. And a person loved by no one has no right to be alive.

She could not say how she knew this, but surely it was self-evident, wasn't it? She knew it because ever since hearing that they did not like her an iron hand had fastened on her heart and was squeezing it to stop it beating. Nothing less than life itself had been closed off. At the very moment of returning from the dead and feeling the life force burning high and bold within her, at that very moment the thing that gives us the right to exist had been snatched from her.

It was worse than a sentence of death, much more brutal than an ordinary sentence of death. She knew what it was like. It was like felling trees, not in the usual way by cutting through the trunk, but by cutting through their roots and letting them stand there and die back slowly. There stands the tree and it cannot understand why it is no longer receiving nourishment. It struggles, it fights for life, but its leaves become smaller, there are no new shoots, and the bark dries and peels. It is bound to die since it has been cut off from the source of life. That is the way of it: it must die.

At last the pedlar from Dalarna set his pack down on the stone slab outside a small cottage deep in the wild forest.

The door of the cottage was locked, but as soon as Ingrid climbed from the sack she found the key under the doorstep, opened the door and went in.

Ingrid was familiar with the cottage and everything in it. It was not the first time she had come there to be comforted. It was not the first time she had come to old Anna Stina and told her that she could not bear it at home any longer, that her foster-mother was so hard on her that she did not want to go back to the manse.

Every time she came the old woman had calmed her down and talked sense into her. She had made dreadful coffee for her, just peas and chicory, with no trace of a coffee bean. But it had been enough to give her courage. And by the end the old woman had made her laugh at it all, had cheered her so much that she had waltzed down the wooded slopes on her way home.

Even if old Anna Stina had been at home to brew her awful coffee it is unlikely to have helped Ingrid this time. But the old woman was down at the manse for Ingrid's funeral, for the minister's wife had not forgotten to invite anyone her foster-daughter had been fond of. That, too, was doubtless a result of her bad conscience.

Everything was as usual in old Anna's cottage. And when Ingrid saw the settle with its wooden seat and the scrubbed and gleaming table and the cat and the coffee-pot, although she certainly did not feel much cheer or comfort, she knew she was in a place where she could give free rein to her grief.

It was a great solace to know that in this place she had no need to think of anything other than her tears and her sorrows.

She immediately went over to the settle, threw herself down on its wooden seat and lay there weeping, she did not know for how long.

Meanwhile the pedlar from Dalarna sat outside on the stone slab, not wanting to go into the cottage because of the cat. He was waiting for Ingrid to come out and play for him. He had taken out the fiddle long before and when time dragged on and she did not come he began to play it himself.

He played gently and softly as he always did and the sound of his playing barely reached the girl.

Ingrid felt one shudder after another pass through her body. She felt as she had done during her illness and she thought she was falling ill again. And it would be a good thing, too, if the fever were to take her and kill her.

When the sound of the fiddle reached her ears she sat up and looked around wild-eyed. Who was playing? Was it her student? Had he come at last?

But she realised immediately that it must be the pedlar from Dalarna and she lay down again with a sigh.

She could not follow what was being played, but the moment she closed her eyes the fiddle took on the voice of the student. She could hear what he was saying; he was talking to her foster-mother and he was defending Ingrid. He talked as beautifully as when he had been talking to Herr and Fru Blomgren. Ingrid needed so much love, he said. That was what she had missed. That was why she had not always done her tasks and had let dreams distract her instead. But no one could even begin to know how she would slave and toil for anyone who loved her. For that person she would shoulder all sorrows and sickness, all scorn and poverty. For that person she would be as strong as a giant and as patient as a slave.

Ingrid could hear clearly what he was saying and a feeling

of calm began to settle over her. How true all of that was. If only her foster-mother had loved her, Ingrid would have shown what she was capable of. But since she had not loved her, Ingrid had been overcome by weakness. That was the truth of it.

No longer aware of the feverish tremors she lay listening to what the student was saying.

And from time to time she must have fallen asleep because in her mind she kept returning to her grave and it was always the student who came and lifted her from her coffin. She lay and argued with him about it.

'Whenever I dream, you are the one who comes,' she said.

'It is always me who comes to help you, Ingrid,' he said. 'You know that. I am the one who raises you from the grave, I am the one who bears you on my shoulders, I am the one who plays you to rest. It is always me.'

What disturbed her and woke her time after time was that she ought to get up and play for the pedlar. Several times she rose intending to do so, but she was too weak.

And as soon as she sank back on the settle she began dreaming that she was crouching in the pack and the student was carrying her through the forest. It was always him.

'But it wasn't you,' she said to him.

'Oh, but it was me,' he said and smiled when she disagreed. 'You have been thinking about me every day for all these years, haven't you? So you must surely see that I had to help you when you were in such danger?'

And she found all of that to be quite self-evident and began to understand that he was right and that it was him.

There seemed to be such infinite bliss in this that she woke once more. Love filled every trembling fibre of her being and could not have been more real if she had seen and been speaking to her dearest and most beloved.

'Why does he never come in reality?' she said half aloud. 'Why does he only come in my dreams?'

She was frightened to move, frightened that the feeling of love would fly away. It was as though a shy bird had come to rest on her shoulder and she was afraid she would frighten it.

If she moved the bird would fly away and sorrow would overcome her.

When at last she woke properly there was the faint light of twilight in the cottage. She must have slept the whole afternoon and evening. At that time of year dusk did not fall before ten o'clock.

The fiddle, too, had stopped playing and the pedlar must have gone on his way.

Old Anna Stina had not yet come home and was presumably intending to stay away for the night.

That did not matter to Ingrid, whose only desire was to lie down and go back to sleep. She was afraid of the sorrow and despair that swept over her whenever she woke up.

But there were other things to think about too. Who had closed the door and covered her with Anna Stina's big shawl? Who had put a piece of bread beside her on the settle?

Billy Goat? Had he really done all that for her?

For a moment she thought she saw dream and reality standing beside one another, each trying to outdo the other in comforting her. Dream stood there sunny and smiling, showering her with the bliss of love to cheer her. But reality, poor, stern and hard, brought its small morsel of kindness to show that it did not mean to treat her as harshly as it had seemed to be doing of late.

VI

Ingrid and old Anna Stina were walking through the dark forest. They had been walking for four days and had slept in shieling huts for three nights. Ingrid was beyond exhaustion, her complexion so pale as to be transparent, her eyes sunken and shining feverishly. Every now and again old Anna Stina would surreptiously cast a worried glance at her and pray to God that He would sustain the girl's strength sufficiently to prevent her sinking and dying on the moss. At times the old woman could not help taking a nervous look behind them: she had an uneasy feeling that Death with his scythe was stalking them through the forest in order to reclaim the girl who had been pledged to him both by the word of the Lord and by the casting of earth on her coffin.

Anna Stina was an old woman, small, broad and with a big square face that had a look of such intelligence that it made her face beautiful. She was not superstitious and she lived alone deep in the forest without fear of trolls or sprites, but as she walked with Ingrid she felt – with as much certainty as if she had been told – that she was walking beside someone who was no longer of this world. The feeling had been with her ever since finding the girl lying in her cottage on the Monday morning.

She had not returned home on Sunday evening because the minister's wife had become dangerously ill and old Anna Stina, who knew how to care for the sick, had stayed to watch over her. She had spent the whole night listening to the woman raving that Ingrid had appeared to her, but the old woman did not believe it.

And when she did get home at last and saw the girl, she

immediately wanted to go back down to the manse and tell them that it was not a ghost they had seen. When she said this to Ingrid, however, the girl had become so distressed that she dared not leave her. Her life had almost flickered out like the flame of a candle in a strong draught. She might have died as easily as a caged bird. Death was pursuing the girl and the only way to keep her alive was to care for her and to proceed very gently.

There was, in fact, so little life left in Ingrid that the old woman was not completely sure whether she was dealing with a ghost or not. She did not attempt to talk sense into her, the only thing to do being to obey her wish that no one should be told she was alive. So the old woman tried to arrange everything as wisely as possible. She had a sister, Stava, who worked as the housekeeper at a big place in Dalarna and she decided to go there, taking Ingrid with her, and to persuade her sister to give Ingrid a place at the manor house. Ingrid would have to be content with a lowly position as a servant, there was no other way.

They were on their way to the manor house now. Old Anna Stina knew the country so well that there had been no need for them to stick to the high road and they had taken lonely forest paths instead. But the going had been hard, the heels of their shoes were worn down, the skirts of their dresses dirty and frayed at the hem, and an ill-disposed twig on a pine tree had torn a long rent in the sleeve of Ingrid's jersey.

In the evening of the fourth day they came out on a wooded hill from which they could look down into a deep valley. There was a lake in the valley and close to the shore was an island on which there stood a white manor house. As soon as Anna Stina saw the house she said it was called Munkhyttan and that was where her sister worked.

While they were still on the hill they tried to make themselves tidy. They retied their headscarves, wiped their shoes with moss and washed in a brook. And old Anna Stina tried to put a tuck in Ingrid's sleeve in order to hide the tear.

But when she looked at Ingrid the old woman sighed and was filled with despair. It was not just that she looked strange in the clothes she had been forced to borrow from the old woman and which did not fit her, but she looked so weak that Stava would surely be reluctant to take her into service. It would be like employing a breath of wind; the girl would be no more useful than a sick butterfly.

Once they were ready they moved on down the hillside towards the lake. It was no distance at all and they were soon approaching the manor house.

And what a manor house it was!

The forest was encroaching on the big neglected fields and filling them with trees. The bridge that led over to the island was so rickety that it seemed unlikely to remain intact for as long as it took them to cross. The avenue running from the bridge to the house was as overgrown with grass as any meadow. And a fallen tree lay right across the road.

There is no doubt that it was beautiful on the island, however, so beautiful that a palace would not have been out of place there. But there was not a single flower growing in the garden and the trees in the great park were so overgrown they were smothering one other. And black grass snakes slithered along the muddy green tracks.

On seeing the state of decay old Anna Stina grew anxious and mumbled to herself as she walked.

'How has this come about? Is my sister Stava dead? How could she let things get like this? It was very different thirty years ago when I was last here. What in Heaven's name is the matter with Stava?' She found it impossible to imagine that this level of disorder could exist in the place where Stava lived.

Ingrid walked slowly and reluctantly behind her. From the moment she set foot on the bridge she had become aware that it was no longer just the two of them present, there were now three.

Someone had come towards her, then turned and was now accompanying her.

She could not hear any footsteps, but she caught glimpses of something close beside her and she was conscious that someone was there.

She was terribly frightened and was about to ask Anna

Stina to turn back, about to say to her that everything here was bewitched and she was afraid to go any further, but before she had time to say anything the stranger came right up to her and she recognised him.

The earlier glimpses had been indistinct, but now that he was clearly visible she could see that it was him, that it was the student.

And now she no longer found it strange and eerie to have him walking with her and, instead, there was something both wonderful and portentous about his coming to meet her. It was as if he were the one who had brought her here and wished to make that known by coming to greet her.

He walked over the bridge with her, and along the avenue, and all the way to the house.

She could not stop herself constantly turning her head to the left in order to steal a look at his face, close beside her cheek. In fact she scarcely saw a face, rather a smile of ineffable beauty that came so caressingly close. But when she actually turned her head fully to look properly there was nothing there. There was nothing, or nothing that was going to allow itself be seen too clearly. But the moment she looked straight ahead, he would appear again close beside her.

He kept her company without speaking. He smiled, that was all, but that was enough for her. It really was quite enough to prove to her that there was someone in the world who held her in love and tenderness.

She felt his presence as something so real that she was utterly convinced he was watching over and protecting her. And the sweet awareness of this swept away all the despair caused by her foster-mother's harsh words.

Ingrid felt she had been returned to life. If someone loved her, she had a right to live.

And so she entered the kitchen at Munkhyttan with a pink glow on her cheeks and a bright gleam in her eye. Delicate still, and weak and translucent, but as beautiful as a newly opened rose.

She was still living in a dream and scarcely knew where she was, but what came as a waking surprise was to see a second

Anna Stina standing over by the stove. Small and broad and with a large square face, just like the first Anna Stina. But so grand! Wearing a white cap tied with ribbons beneath her chin and a dress of black bombasine. Ingrid's head was still so dizzy and confused that it took her some time to realise that this must be Stava, the housekeeper.

She could feel old Anna Stina's worried eyes fixed on her and she tried to pull herself together to greet Stava. But the only thing that mattered to her was that he had come.

There was a tiny little room off the kitchen and everything in it was done in blue check. Stava led them in there and gave them food and coffee.

Anna Stina immediately began explaining why they had come. She talked for a long time and she said that she knew that her ladyship, the widow of the inspector of mines, had such great confidence in Stava that she left it to her to engage servants for the estate. The housekeeper said nothing in reply, but the look she gave the girl was enough to reveal that she would not have earned that trust if she had chosen servants like Ingrid.

Anna Stina praised Ingrid, saying what a good girl she was. Until now she had been in service in a manse, but now that she was grown up she wished to learn a proper skill, which is why old Anna Stina had wanted to bring her to the person who could teach her more than anyone else she knew.

The housekeeper Stava still did not respond. But the looks she gave did nothing to conceal the fact that she was wondering why a girl who had been in service in a manse had no clothes of her own and had needed to borrow them from an old woman like Anna Stina.

Anna Stina then began to describe the kind of life she herself led, living all alone in the forest deserted by all her relations. But then there was this young lass who had often come running up the hill to visit during the evening or early morning and that was why she was hoping to arrange for her to get a good position.

The housekeeper said it was a pity they had come such a long way to find a place. If the girl was a capable girl surely she could have gone into service at a big house in their own district?

Old Anna Stina realised now that things were not going too well and she began to address Stava in a more lofty tone.

'You have spent your whole life here in great comfort and prosperity, Stava, while I have had to struggle with considerable poverty. Until today I have never asked you for anything. And now you are quite prepared to let me depart like a beggar woman to whom you have given some food and nothing else!'

Stava the housekeeper gave a little smile and said:

'You're not telling me the truth, sister. I come from Råglanda, too, and what I would like to know is which peasant cottage in that parish is capable of producing a face and eyes such as this girl has?'

She pointed at Ingrid before continuing:

'I do understand, Anna Stina, why you might want to help someone who looks like that, but you must think I've gone so soft in the head that you can come here and lie to me.'

This came as such a surprise to Anna Stina that she was lost for words, so Ingrid decided to confide in the old housekeeper and speaking in a low and attractive voice she began to tell her story.

Ingrid had scarcely said more than a few words about how she had been lying in her grave until the Dalarna man came and rescued her before the old housekeeper's face flushed and she quickly bent down to hide it. It did not last more than a moment but it must nevertheless have signified something good because from then on her expression was friendly.

And now she quickly began asking very detailed questions about the whole business and, in particular, she wanted to hear about the madman and whether Ingrid had been afraid of him or not.

'Oh no! He wasn't in the least dangerous. Nor was he stupid,' Ingrid said, 'because he was capable of both buying and selling. He was just very frightened.'

The hardest part for Ingrid was having to tell what she had heard her foster-mother saying. But she recounted it all truthfully even though it brought a sob to her throat.

Then Stava went over to her, pushed back her head-scarf and looked her in the eye. She patted her gently on the cheek.

'You can leave all that out, Miss, if you want to,' she said. 'I don't need to know that. And now, dear sister, you and Miss Ingrid will have to excuse me because I have to take madam her coffee. I'll come back quickly and hear the rest.'

When she returned, however, she said she had told the inspector's widow about the young girl and the grave. And now her mistress wanted to see the girl.

They were taken upstairs to the upper floor where the inspector's widow had a small drawing room. Old Anna Stina stayed by the door but Ingrid did not feel shy and immediately walked over to the old lady and took her hand. She had been shy with other people who looked far less grand, but she was not shy in this house. She felt so inexpressibly happy to have come here.

'So this is the child who was buried,' the inspector's widow said, nodding to her in a kindly way. 'Do please tell me the whole story, little friend. I'm all alone here, you know, and I never hear anything.'

And Ingrid began once again to tell her story. She had not gone very far before being interrupted. The lady did precisely the same as her housekeeper had done: she stood up, pushed Ingrid's scarf back from her face and looked her in the eyes.

'Oh yes,' she said, speaking to herself. 'I can understand it. I can understand him obeying these eyes.'

And for the first time in her life Ingrid was praised for her courage. The lady thought she had been very courageous to risk trusting herself to a madman.

Ingrid said she would probably have been frightened of him had she not been even more afraid that people would see her in the state she was in. And he was not dangerous, he was almost sane, and he was so kind.

The lady wanted to know what he was called, but Ingrid did not know. The only name she had heard was Billy Goat.

And now the inspector's widow asked her several times about how he behaved when he went round selling things.

Had she laughed at him? Did she think he looked dreadful, this Billy Goat? It sounded very strange to hear the lady say the words Billy Goat. She pronounced them with dreadful bitterness, yet she said them time after time.

No, Ingrid did not think any such thing. Nor was she in the habit of laughing at those who were unfortunate.

The expression on the lady's face was gentler than her words sounded. 'You must understand madmen really well, little friend,' she said. 'That's a great gift. Most people are afraid of poor wretches like that.'

She listened to Ingrid's story right to the end and then sat in thought.

'As you have no other home,' she said, 'I should like to ask you to stay with me. I am an old woman all alone here and you could keep me company. I shall see to it that you have all you need. Would you be happy with that, little friend?'

'The time might come,' the lady continued, 'when we have to inform your parents that you are alive, but for the moment we'll leave everything as it is to give you time to find peace with yourself. Now you must call me aunt, my dear, but what shall I call you?'

'Ingrid – Ingrid Berg.'

'Ingrid,' the lady said thoughtfully. 'I would rather call you something else. The moment you entered the room with those starry eyes of yours I thought you should be called Mignon.'

Now that the girl understood that she was to be given a real home here she became more certain than ever that there was something supernatural about the way she had been brought here. She whispered a silent word of thanks to her invisible protector even before she thanked the inspector's widow, the housekeeper Stava and old Anna Stina.

*

Ingrid lay in a four-poster bed, resting on a feather mattress several feet thick. The sheet had a wide hemstitched edge and the silk coverlet was embroidered with Swedish crowns and French lilies. The bed was so wide that she could lie as she liked, both crosswise and lengthwise, and it was so high she had to climb two steps to reach it. High up on the ceiling there was a Cupid from which colourful curtains hung down over her, and other Cupids on the bedposts were used to drape the curtains in swathes.

In the same room there was an old bow-fronted chest of drawers, inlaid with lemonwood, and from it Ingrid could take all the fragrant white linen she wanted. There was also a cupboard in which there hung many beautiful and colourful silk and muslin dresses waiting for her to choose which one she would like to wear.

When she woke in the morning she found a gleaming silver coffee tray laid with old East Indies porcelain beside her. And every morning she sank her small white teeth into fine white wheaten bread and wonderful almond bun. Every day she dressed in a light muslin dress with a fichu tied at the back. She wore her hair high at the nape of her neck but with a fringe of tight ringlets around her forehead.

There was a mirror fixed on the wall between the windows. The glass was narrow and the frame was broad and she would look at herself in it, nod at the reflection and ask: 'Is it you, is it really you? How did you get here?'

In the daytime when Ingrid left the room with the great bed she would sit in the elegant drawing room stitching tambour embroidery or painting silk. When she tired of that she would pluck the guitar, sing little songs and chat to the inspector's widow, who taught her French and took pleasure in training her to be a fine lady.

But there could be no doubt that a spell had been cast on this manor house and she found it impossible to forget that. She had felt the place was bewitched from the very first moment and that thought returned to her time after time.

No one came and no one left. Only a few of the rooms in this great house were occupied, the rest were never used. No one walked in the garden and no one tended it. The estate had only one worker, along with an old man who chopped wood. And Stava had only two maids to help her in the kitchen and in the cowshed.

But there was always fine food and the inspector's widow and Ingrid always dressed like elegant ladies and were served at table.

Though little else may have flourished at the old manor there can be no doubt it provided fertile soil for dreams. Other plants may not have been cultivated but Ingrid certainly tended her dream roses. Every moment she had to herself they grew around her and she felt that her red dream roses were forming a canopy over her.

Round the island, where the trees bent low over the water and sent long branches out among the reeds, where bushes and plants flourished in abundance, there was a path that Ingrid often walked. She found it strange to see trees with so many letters carved into them, to see old seats and benches and even old decaying pavilions with floors so rotten she did not dare step on them. To think that there used to be people here, used to be life and dreams and love, that the manor had not always been under a spell.

The path was where the spell was at its strongest. That was where the smiling face appeared to her. That was where she could walk and thank him, thank the student for allowing her to come here, to a place where she was so happy and so loved that it made her forget how harsh others had been to her.

Had it not been for him arranging things it would have been impossible for her to stay here, quite impossible.

She knew, of course, that it must be him. She had never had such wild thoughts before: she had always thought of him but she had never felt that he was near her, that he had taken care of her.

The only thing she still wondered about was when he would come – because come he certainly would. It was impossible that he would not come. He had left a part of his soul among these avenues.

*

Summer passed and autumn too. Christmas was approaching.

'Miss Ingrid,' the housekeeper said one day in a rather mysterious tone, 'I think you should know that the young master who owns the estate will be coming home for Christmas. At least, he usually does,' she added with a sigh.

'Madam has never mentioned a son!' Ingrid said.

But she was not in the least surprised. In fact, she would have liked to say that she had known the whole time.

'No one has mentioned anything about him to you before,' Stava said, 'because madam has forbidden us to talk about him.'

And Stava the housekeeper would say no more than that.

Nor did Ingrid want to ask her more. She was nervous about hearing anything really definite. She had built her hopes so high that she was afraid they would collapse. Truth could be sweet to know, but it could also be bitter and lay waste all her beautiful dreams.

From then on, however, he was close to her night and day. She scarcely found time to speak to anyone else. She had to be with him constantly.

One day she noticed that the avenue had been cleared of snow. She was almost afraid. Was he coming now?

The following day the inspector's widow sat by the window from morning onwards, watching the road. Ingrid sat farther back in the room, too nervous to sit by the window.

'Do you know who I am expecting today, Ingrid?' she asked suddenly.

The girl just nodded, unable to trust her voice to speak.

'Has Stava told you that my son is strange?'

Ingrid shook her head.

'He is very strange ... he ... I can't talk about it, I just can't ... You'll see for yourself.'

It sounded heart-rending and it shook Ingrid to the core. What was it that made everything so strange on this estate? Was there something dreadful she did not know about? Were mother and son enemies? What was it? What was it?

At one moment ecstatic happiness, at the next a fever of doubt! She had to call to mind all her visions in order to reassure herself that he must be the one who was coming.

She simply could not explain why she was so certain that he would be none other than the son of the house she was now living in. For all she knew he could well be someone else. Oh Lord Above, how hard it was never to have heard his name!

It was a long day. They sat waiting in unbroken silence until evening came.

Then the farmhand drove up with a cartload of logs for Christmas. He left the horse standing in the courtyard while the logs were being unloaded.

'Ingrid,' the inspector's widow said in a forceful and commanding voice, 'run down and tell Anders to take the horse away! At once! At once!'

The girl rushed down the stairs and out onto the veranda. But when she got there she forgot to call to the farmhand, for just behind the cart she saw a tall man in a white sheepskin coat with a great pack on his back. She did not have to see the way he stood there bobbing, forever bobbing, in order to recognise him.

'But, but …' She put her hand to her forehead and took a deep breath. How was she ever to understand all this? Was it because of this man that madam had sent her down? And why was the farmhand taking the horse away in such haste? And why had he removed his cap when he greeted the man? What did the people at the manor have to do with the madman?

Then the truth came to Ingrid, and it came with such crushing force that she could have screamed. It was not her beloved who had been watching over her, it was this madman. She had been allowed to stay here because she had spoken well of him, because his mother had wanted to complete the good deed he had started.

The madman, the Billy Goat – he was the young master.

No one was going to come to her, no one had led her, no one had expected her. They were just dreams, fancies, illusions.

She felt such bitterness. If only she had never expected it to be him.

But at night, when Ingrid was lying in the great bed with its colourful curtains, she dreamt time after time that she saw the student coming home.

'It wasn't you who came,' she said then.

'Yes, of course it was me,' he answered, and in her dream she believed him.

VII

It was one day during the week after Christmas and Ingrid was sitting by the window in the small drawing room working at her tambour embroidery. The inspector's widow was sitting on the sofa knitting, as she always did now. The room was completely silent.

Young Hede had been home for a week and Ingrid had not met him during that time. Even in his own home he lived like a peasant, sleeping in the farmhand's bothy and eating in the kitchen. He never came up to his mother.

Ingrid knew that his mother and Stava were both expecting her to do something for Hede, expecting her at least to try to persuade him to stay at home. And it grieved her that she found it impossible to do what they desired. She was filled with despair at the sense of powerlessness that had come over her since the collapse of all her hopes.

Stava the housekeeper had just come into the room and told them that Hede was filling his pack ready to leave. This time he was not even staying as long as he usually stayed during his Christmas visits, Stava said, giving Ingrid a reproachful look.

Ingrid knew what they had been expecting of her but she had been unable to do anything. She carried on with her work and said nothing.

Stava went out and the room fell silent again. Ingrid quite forgot that she was not alone and she suddenly fell into a kind of trance, in which all her sad thoughts formed themselves into a vision.

She imagined herself walking through the whole of the great manor house. She passed through salons and rooms and rooms and salons and she saw furniture wrapped in grey dust-sheets, paintings and chandeliers covered over with gauze and the floor coated with a thick layer of dust that swirled up as she walked. At last she came to a room she had never been in before, quite a small room in which the ceiling and walls were black. But when she looked more closely she saw that the room was not painted black, nor was it swathed in black cloth. The reason it was so dark was that myriads of bats were hanging from the ceiling and the walls. The whole room was nothing but a huge bat roost. There was a pane missing from the window so it was easy to see how the creatures had been able to enter in such numbers that they filled the whole room. Now they were hanging there in hibernation, motionless, not one of them moving as she entered.

She, however, was seized by such horror at the sight that she began to shudder and shake. There was something horrible about this great mass of creatures she could see hanging there. All of them had their black wings wrapped around them like cloaks, all of them had driven a single long black claw into the wall and were hanging from it, sleeping the most profound and motionless sleep.

She saw it all so clearly that she wondered whether the housekeeper Stava knew that a whole room had been taken over by bats.

In her imagination she went to Stava and asked her whether she had been into this room and seen all the creatures.

'Of course I've seen them,' the housekeeper said. 'It's their room. Surely Miss Ingrid knows that there's not a single old manor in the country that does not have a room left aside for bats?'

'I've never heard of such a thing before,' Ingrid said.

'When you've been in this world as long as I have, Miss, you'll see that I'm telling the truth,' Stava said.

'I can't understand how anyone could tolerate something like that,' Ingrid said.

'We have no choice,' Stava said. 'Those bats are the birds of Lady Sorrow and it is at her command that we receive them here.'

Ingrid could see that the housekeeper did not want to say any more about it and so she went back to her embroidery, but she could not stop thinking about Lady Sorrow. Who could she be, who had such power here that she could force the housekeeper to open up a room for bats?

No sooner had she had that thought than she saw a covered sledge, all black and drawn by black horses, drive up to the veranda.

She saw Stava the housekeeper go out and make a deep curtsey. Out of the sledge stepped an old woman wearing a long black velvet cloak with many small capes over her shoulders. Her back was very bent and she had difficulty walking. She was scarcely able to lift her feet high enough to climb the steps.

'Ingrid,' the inspector's widow said, looking up from her knitting. 'I think I heard Lady Sorrow arrive. That must have been the tinkling of her bell. Have you noticed that her horses never wear sleigh bells, just the one tiny little bell? But you can hear it anyway, oh, how you can hear it! Go down to the hall, Ingrid, and welcome Lady Sorrow!'

When Ingrid went down to the hall she found Lady Sorrow talking to Stava the housekeeper on the veranda. They did not notice Ingrid.

Ingrid was astonished to see that the bent old lady was hiding something under all the shoulder capes, something that resembled black crape. It was carefully tucked in and well hidden. Ingrid had to look very carefully before discovering that what Lady Sorrow was attempting to conceal was a pair of big leathery bat wings. This made the girl even more curious about Lady Sorrow than she had been before and she tried to see her face, but it was impossible because she was standing facing the courtyard. What Ingrid did see, however, when the woman raised her hand towards the housekeeper, was that one finger was much longer than the others and ended in a long crooked claw.

'Everything is as usual on the estate?' she said.

'Yes, your Ladyship,' the housekeeper answered.

'You haven't planted any flowers or trees? You haven't

mended the bridge or cleared the weeds from the avenue?'

'No, your Ladyship.'

'That is precisely how things should be,' Lady Sorrow said. 'And you haven't risked trying to locate the seam of iron ore or cutting back the forest where it is encroaching on the fields, have you?'

'No, your Ladyship.'

'Nor cleared out the wells?'

'No, we haven't cleared the wells.'

'This is a good place,' Lady Sorrow said. 'I feel at home here. In a few years my birds will be able to occupy the whole house. You are kind to my birds, you are.'

The housekeeper curtseyed humbly on hearing these words of praise.

'How are things in other respects?' Lady Sorrow asked. 'How did you celebrate Christmas?'

'We celebrated it in our usual way,' Stava said. 'Madam stays quietly indoors, knitting day in and day out. She thinks of nothing but her son and doesn't even know it is Christmas. Christmas Eve passes like any other day and there are no gifts and no candles.'

'No Christmas tree, no Christmas food?'

'No church, either, your Ladyship. Not even candles in the windows on Christmas morning.'

'Why should a widow celebrate God's son when God won't heal her son?' Lady Sorrow said.

'No, why should she?'

'He has been home again, I imagine. Perhaps he is better now?'

'No, he is no better. He is as terrified of everything as he always was.'

'Is he still behaving like a peasant? Will he still not come into the house?'

'We cannot get him into the house – he is afraid of his mother, as your Ladyship knows.'

'He eats in the kitchen and sleeps in the farmhand's bothy?'

'Yes, he does.'

'And you have no idea how to make him better?'

'We don't know anything and we don't understand anything.'

Lady Sorrow fell silent for a moment. When she began speaking again her voice had a hard and sharp edge to it.

'All of which may indeed be very well, Stava, but I am still not really pleased with you.'

And at the same moment she turned round and fixed her eyes sharply on Ingrid's face.

Ingrid recoiled. Lady Sorrow had a small, furrowed face, the lower part so pinched that her jaw was scarcely visible. Her teeth were like the teeth of a saw and her upper lip very hairy. Each eyebrow was a single tuft and her skin was all brown.

Ingrid wondered whether the housekeeper was seeing what she was seeing. Lady Sorrow was not a human being, she was an animal.

Lady Sorrow opened her lips so that her gleaming teeth could be seen as she looked at Ingrid.

'When she came here, this girl,' she said to Stava, 'you all thought she had been sent to you. You saw in her eyes that she had been sent in order to save him. She had a way with madmen. So, how did it go?'

'It didn't. She hasn't done anything at all.'

'No, I was the one who saw to that,' Lady Sorrow said. 'I was the one who made sure you didn't tell her why she was permitted to stay here. If she had known that she would not have indulged herself in rosy hopes of meeting the one she loved. And if she had not indulged in such hopes she would not have suffered such dreadful disappointment. And if that disappointment had not paralysed her she would perhaps have been able to do something for the madman. But as things are she hasn't bothered about him. She hates him because he is not the one he should be. That is my doing, all my doing, Stava.'

'Your Ladyship knows her business,' Stava said.

Lady Sorrow took out a lace handkerchief and dried her red-rimmed eyes. It seemed to be a gesture of satisfaction.

'You do not need to pretend, Stava,' she said. 'You don't like me taking over that room for my birds, do you? You don't like the fact that I shall soon take over the whole house, I know that. You and your mistress intended to deceive me. But that's in the past now.'

'Yes,' the housekeeper said, 'your Ladyship can rest easy. It's in the past. The young master leaves today. He has packed his pack, so we can be sure he is leaving. Everything that his mother and I dreamt throughout the autumn is in the past now. Nothing has come of it. We believed that she would at least have been able to tempt him to stay at home, but in spite of all the good things we have done for her she has done nothing for us.'

'She has been of no use, I know that,' Lady Sorrow said. 'But she must go now anyway. That is what I want to talk to your mistress about.'

Lady Sorrow began dragging herself on her unsteady legs up the stairs to the upper floor. With every step she opened her wings a little to help. There is no doubt she would have much preferred to fly.

Ingrid followed her. In some strange way she was both attracted and under a spell. The urge to follow her would not have been stronger even if she had been the most beautiful woman in the world.

When Ingrid entered the small drawing room Lady Sorrow was sitting on the sofa beside the inspector's widow and whispering confidentially in her ear as though they were dear old friends.

'You must surely understand that you can't keep her here with you,' Lady Sorrow was saying in an ingratiating voice. 'You, who cannot even tolerate a flower in your garden, surely can't put up with having a young girl about the house. Someone like that is always bound to bring a little joy and jollity and that wouldn't suit you, would it?'

'No, I was just sitting here thinking that.'

'Find her a position as a lady's companion somewhere else, but don't keep her here!'

She rose to bid farewell.

'That was all I wanted to say to you,' she said. 'Apart from that, how are you?'

'Knives and scissors stab my heart all day long,' the inspector's widow answered. 'I live through him as long as he is at home. It's worse than usual, far worse this time. I can't bear it any longer.'

Madam's bell rang and Ingrid jumped. She had been sitting there with her imagination working so powerfully that she was amazed to find that the inspector's widow was alone and there was no black sledge at the door.

Madam had rung to summon the housekeeper, but Stava did not come, so she asked Ingrid to go down to her room and fetch her.

Ingrid went, but she found the little blue-checked room empty. She was about to go to the kitchen and ask where Stava was, but before she opened the door she heard Hede's voice. She stood still, unable to bring herself to meet him.

And then she tried to overcome her reluctance. He could not help not being the one she was expecting. She ought to try to do something for him. She ought try to persuade him to stay at home. She had not felt any dislike of him before. He was not really that dreadful, was he?

She bent down and looked through the keyhole.

Hede was sitting at the table eating. What was happening here was the same as happened everywhere else – the kitchen maids were chatting with him just to hear his peculiar speech.

Now they were asking him who he was going to marry.

Hede smiled. He was very pleased to be asked a question like that.

'She is called Grave-Lily, you know that, don't you?' he said.

No, the kitchen maid had not known that she had such a fine name.

'Where does she live then?'

'She has no home and she has no farm,' Hede said. 'She lives in my pack.'

The maid said that was an unusual place to live, that was, and then she asked about Grave-Lily's parents.

'She has no father and she has no mother,' Hede said. 'She is as beautiful as a flower and she grew in a garden.'

Up to this point he had spoken with reasonable clarity, but

when he tried to describe how beautiful his beloved was he was no longer able to make sense. A host of words poured out, all strangely muddled. It became impossible to follow his train of thought although his speech obviously gave him great pleasure. He sat there beaming and smiling.

Ingrid hurried away. She could not bear it. There was nothing she could do for him. She found him repulsive.

She had gone no farther than the staircase before her conscience pricked her again. She had received so much kindness here and yet she was unwilling to give anything in return.

In an effort to overcome her disgust she tried to imagine Hede as a gentleman. What must he have looked like in fine clothes and with his hair swept back? She closed her eyes for a moment and considered it. No, it was impossible! She could not see him as anyone other than the man he was.

At that moment, however, she saw the outlines of a beloved face close beside her, hovering to her left and wonderfully distinct.

The face was not smiling now. Its lips were trembling in pain and there was terrible suffering inscribed in the sharp lines at the corners of the mouth.

Ingrid stood still on the staircase and looked at it. It was there, fleeting and light, no more tangible than a sunspot thrown by the cut glass of a chandelier, but just as visible, just as real. She thought of the vision she had just had, but this was not like that. This was reality.

After she had watched the face for a while its lips began to move and it spoke, but she could not hear a sound. Then she tried to see what it was saying, tried to read the words from the lips as deaf people do. And she succeeded.

'Do not let me go!' the lips said. 'Do not let me go!'

And it was said with such anguish! If someone had been lying at her feet begging for life it could not have affected her more profoundly. She was so moved that she shook. She had never experienced anything so heart-rending in all her life. She would never have believed that anyone could beg with such infinite anguish.

Time after time the lips begged: 'Do not let me go!' And the anguish grew greater each time.

Ingrid understood nothing, she simply stood there motionless in the grip of indescribable pity.

For someone to beg like this, she thought, it must be about something more than life, it must be about nothing short of the salvation of his soul.

The lips had ceased moving and hung half open in weary despair.

And when they assumed this dull expression, she gave a little cry and staggered several steps down the staircase, for she recognised the face of the madman, just as she had seen it a little time before.

'No, no, no!' she said. 'It cannot be, it must not be, it just cannot be! It cannot possibly be him!'

At that moment the face vanished.

For what was perhaps a whole hour she remained sitting on the cold staircase weeping in hopeless despair. But hope did come to her at last – bright, uplifting hope.

Everything that had happened pointed to her being the one to save him. That was why she had been brought there. She was the one who would have the great, great happiness of saving him.

Back in the small drawing room the inspector's widow was talking to Stava the housekeeper. It was pitiful to hear her begging Stava to persuade her son to stay a few more days.

The housekeeper seemed harsh and stern.

'We can certainly ask him, but you know, madam, that no one can get him to stay any longer than he wants.'

'But we have enough money. There is no need at all for him to leave. Can't you say to him, Gustava …?'

Ingrid came in at that moment. She opened the door silently and slipped through the room with light airy steps. Her eyes gleamed as if they were looking at something wondrous but far off.

When the inspector's widow saw her she frowned slightly. She was seized by an urge to be cruel in her turn, to cause pain in her turn.

'Come here, Ingrid,' she said. 'I must talk to you about your future.'

The girl had come to fetch her guitar and was now about to leave the room. She turned to the inspector's widow.

'About my future ...?' she said, passing her hand across her brow. 'My future has already been decided, you know,' she continued with a small smile of martyrdom. And then, without saying anything more, she left the room.

The inspector's widow and the housekeeper looked at one another in astonishment. Then they began to discuss where to send the girl.

But when the housekeeper went down to her room Ingrid was sitting there, plucking her guitar and singing little songs. Sitting opposite her and listening with a face that was all sunshine was Hede.

VIII

From the moment Ingrid recognised that the madman was Gunnar Hede her only thought was how to heal him. But it was a difficult task and she had no idea how to set about it.

To begin with she simply thought of persuading him to stay at home. That proved quite easy – just the chance to hear her play the fiddle or the guitar for a little while every day led him to sit patiently in Stava's room waiting for Ingrid from morning to night.

She felt it would be a great thing if she could convince him to go into the other rooms, but his courage failed him. She tried shutting herself away and saying that he would not hear her play until he came and joined her. But after she had stayed away for two days he began to pack his things to leave and she was forced to give in.

He had a great affection for her, clearly preferring her to all the others, but he was unable to let go of any of his fear and pass it over to her.

She asked him to give up his sheepskin coat and wear an ordinary coat. He did so at once but she found him wearing it again the following day. When she hid it from him he appeared wearing the farmhand's sheepskin, so it was better to let him wear his own.

He was still as frightened as ever and very careful not to let anyone come too close. Not even Ingrid was allowed to sit close beside him.

One day she told him that there was something he must promise her. He must stop bobbing to the cat. She was not asking him to do anything really difficult like not curtseying to horses and dogs, but surely he could not be afraid of a little cat.

'Oh yes I am,' he said. 'The cat is a billy goat.'

'But it can't be a billy goat or a nanny goat,' she said. 'After all, it doesn't have any horns.' This pleased him enormously. It was as if he had at last found a way of distinguishing goats from other animals.

The following day he happened to see the housekeeper's cat.

'That goat hasn't got any horns,' he said laughing proudly. He walked past it and sat down on the sofa to listen to Ingrid playing. But after a short while he grew restless, stood up, walked over to the cat and gave a bob.

Ingrid was in despair. She took him by the arm and shook him. He immediately ran out and did not reappear until the following day.

'Dear child,' the inspector's widow said, 'you are doing what I do, you are trying my way, but you will frighten him and then he'll be afraid to see you. Better to leave him in peace. We are happy with things as they are, just as long as he stays at home.'

There was nothing she could do apart from sit and wring her hands in sorrow for the fine, lovable man hidden within this madman.

Ingrid would have liked to know if she had been brought here for no other purpose than to play her grandfather's tunes to him and nothing else. Was this how they were to spend the rest of their lives? Would things never change?

She used to tell him stories, too, and in the middle of a story his face might suddenly light up and he would say something strangely wonderful and beautiful to her, the kind of thing someone in their right mind would never have been able to come up with. And that was all it took to give her renewed courage and to set them off again on their unending efforts.

*

It was late one afternoon and the moon was rising. The snow lay white on the ground and the lake was covered with gleaming grey ice. The trees were dark brown and the sunset sky was flaming red.

Ingrid was on her way to the lake to skate, following a narrow path where the snow had been trampled flat. Gunnar Hede was walking behind her. There was something cowed in his bearing, something that put you in mind of a dog following its master.

Ingrid looked tired. There was no brightness in her eyes and her complexion was ashen.

As she walked she began to wonder whether the day that was drawing to a close was pleased with itself. Was it in jubilation that the day had kindled that great fiery red sunset away in the west?

For her part she knew she could not light a fire in celebration of that day or of any other day. During the whole month that had passed since she recognised Gunnar Hede she had achieved nothing.

But today she had been seized by profound anxiety. It was as if she were wasting her love on all this. She was beginning to forget the student and think only of the sick man. All that was light and lovely and playful in her love was disappearing and what was left was dull and heavy and earnest.

As she walked towards the lake she was despairing. She felt that she had no understanding of what needed to be done, felt that she would have to give up. O God in Heaven! Here was Hede, walking behind her looking so strong and healthy and yet so helplessly and incurably afflicted.

They were down beside the lake and she was putting on her skates. She was trying to get him to come too and she put his skates on, but he fell over as soon as he stepped onto the ice. He crawled ashore and sat on a rock while she skated away from him.

Directly in front of the rock on which Gunnar Hede was sitting there was a small island, overgrown with birch and aspen trees that were now leafless. Behind the island the evening sky still glowed a fierce red and it was impossible not to see how beautiful the outline of the slender leafless treetops was against this redness.

It seems to be a truth that we recognise places by some particular feature, because even with the places we know best we cannot really know what they look like from all sides and angles. In the case of Munkhyttan it was this little island that was most immediately recognisable. People who had not seen the estate for many years recognised it by the island lying out there with its dark treetops reaching up towards the sunset.

Hede sat motionless gazing at the island and the slim branches of the trees and the grey ice that spread out in all directions.

This was a scene he knew better than any other. There was nothing on the whole estate he knew as well as he knew this. The island never failed to draw people's eyes and soon Hede was sitting there looking at the island, but without even thinking about it. Which is what people tend to do when they know something very well. He sat and stared for a long time and there was nothing to disturb him – no people, no wind, nothing strange. He could not see Ingrid because she had sped far away across the ice.

And now peace and rest came to Gunnar Hede, the kind of peace and rest that only comes to those who feel thoroughly at home. A sense of security and calm flowed through him from that small island and stilled the constant unrest that had been tormenting him.

Hede believed that he was forever surrounded by enemies and consequently he thought he must always be on his guard. It was many years since he had felt the kind of peace that allowed him to forget himself, but now it came to him.

As he sat there thinking of nothing at all it so happened that he began to function mechanically, as people do when they are in familiar surroundings. He was sitting there, the ice was in front of him and he was wearing skates, so he stood up and began to skate out on the lake. And he thought no more about what he was doing than he would have thought about using a knife and fork to eat.

He glided out over the surface of the ice, which was in the best possible condition for skating, and he was far from the shore before he became aware of what he was doing.

'What wonderful ice,' he thought, 'I wonder why I didn't come out earlier today.'

Then he comforted himself: 'I had lots of time out here yesterday, though, and I must make sure I don't miss a day for the rest of the vacation.'

What must have occurred was this: because Gunnar Hede happened to do something he had been in the habit of doing before he became ill, aspects of his former self had stirred. Thoughts and perceptions that were part of his old life forced themselves to the surface of his consciousness and all thoughts connected with his illness sank into oblivion.

As he had always done when out skating he made a wide sweep across the lake so that he could see past a pointed headland. He did it unconsciously, but once he had passed the headland he remembered that he made that wide sweep in order to be able to see if there were lights in his mother's window.

'She'll be thinking it's about time for me to come in, but she can wait a while yet. The ice is too good.'

But what mainly stirred within him were vague feelings of joy at his own movements and at the beauty of the evening. A beautiful moonlit evening like this was exactly the right time to go skating. He loved the gentle transition from day to night. There was still some light but peace was already spreading. All that was best of both day and night.

There was one other skater on the ice. A young girl. He did not know whether he knew her, but he steered towards her to find out. No, it was no one he knew, but he could not avoid saying a few words about the excellent quality of the ice as he passed her.

The stranger must surely be a girl from the town, he thought, since she was obviously not accustomed to being spoken to without introduction. She had looked very frightened when he addressed a few words to her. But, then, he did look rather strange, dressed from head to foot in peasant clothes.

Well, he had no intention of frightening her away. He

turned and skated further up the lake. There was plenty of ice for both of them.

But Ingrid had very nearly uttered a scream of astonishment. He had come skating towards her, handsome and elegant, his arms folded across his chest, the brim of his hat turned up and his hair swept back so that it did not fall over his ears.

His voice had been that of an educated man, with scarcely a trace of a Dalarna accent.

She did not waste time wondering about it, but set off at once for the shore.

She ran breathlessly into the kitchen. She did not know how best to tell them so that they would understand clearly.

'Stava, Stava, the young master has come home!'

But the kitchen was empty and both housekeeper and maids were out. Nor was there anyone in the housekeeper's room. Ingrid ran through the whole house, rushing into rooms that no one usually entered. And the whole time she was calling: 'Stava, Stava, the young master has come home!'

She was quite beside herself and still shouting when she reached the first-floor landing and joined the two maids, Stava the housekeeper and the inspector's widow herself. She repeated the same words time after time, too overwrought to be able to stop.

But none of them misunderstood what she meant. All four of them stood there as overwhelmed as she was, their faces working and their hands trembling.

Ingrid turned desperately from one to another. She felt she ought to be providing explanations and giving orders, but what orders? Oh, why did she have to lose her presence of mind like this! She gave the inspector's widow a frantically questioning look. What was it I wanted? What was it?

The old lady issued some commands in a quiet and unsteady voice – almost a whisper, in fact.

'Candles and a fire in the young master's room! His clothes must be laid out!'

It was hardly the time and place for Stava to put on airs but there was more than a hint of pride in her voice when she answered.

'There is always a fire in the young master's room. And his clothes are always laid out ready for him.'

'Ingrid, you should go to your room,' madam said.

The girl did quite the opposite. She went into the drawing room and stood by the window, quite unconscious of the fact she was sobbing and shaking.

Impatiently she wiped away the tears from her eyes so that she could watch the snowfield that lay in front of the house. As long as there were no tears in her eyes nothing would escape her in the clear moonlight outside. And then he came.

'There! There!' she shouted to the inspector's widow. 'He is walking quickly! He is running! Just come and look.'

His mother, however, remained motionless in front of the fire. She did not move. She concentrated on listening, just as Ingrid did on looking.

She bade Ingrid to be quiet so that she could hear how he was walking. Yes, oh yes, she would be quiet so that his mother could hear how he was walking! She gripped the window-frame tightly as though that would help her. 'You must be quiet,' she whispered to herself, 'so that she can hear him walking.'

Her Ladyship was leaning forward, listening as though her life depended on it. Were those his footsteps she could hear out in the yard? She was naturally expecting him to turn into the kitchen, but surely the creaks she could hear were coming from the main staircase? The door that was being opened was the door to the hall, wasn't it? Could she hear how quickly the footsteps were coming up the staircase to the upper floor? Two or three steps at a time! Had his mother noticed that? This was not the heavy trudging peasant gait with which he had left the house.

Hearing him approach the door of the drawing room gave them a fright. There is no doubt they would have screamed if he had come in.

But he turned aside and crossed the landing towards his own rooms.

His mother sank back in her chair and closed her eyes. It

seemed to Ingrid that her Ladyship would have liked to die just at that moment.

Without opening her eyes she reached out her hand and Ingrid moved quietly forward and took it. She drew Ingrid close to her:

'Mignon,' she said, 'Mignon. It was the right name after all.'

'No,' she continued. 'We mustn't cry now. We mustn't talk about this just now. Pull up the footstool and sit by the fire. We must keep calm, little friend. Let's talk about something else. We must be utterly calm when he comes.'

When Hede came in half an hour later there was tea on the table and the candles in the chandelier had been lighted. He had changed his clothes and he looked like a gentleman. Ingrid and his mother held hands very tightly.

They had been sitting trying to get used to the idea of seeing him. It was impossible to imagine what he might say or do. His mother had said he had always been unpredictable, but whatever happened the two of them must stay calm.

And Ingrid really had become calm. An infinite sense of bliss overwhelmed her and calmed her. It was as if she was ascending to all the blessings of Heaven with an untroubled mind, resting in the bosom of angels who were carrying her ever higher.

Hede himself did not seem in the least confused.

'I've only come in,' he said, 'to say that I have such a severe headache that I must go and lie down at once. I felt it coming on while I was out on the ice.'

His mother did not say anything in response. It was all so simple, but it would have been quite impossible for her to imagine it. It took her a moment or two to get used to the idea that he knew nothing of his illness, that he was living at some point in the past.

'But perhaps I might take a cup of tea first anyway,' he said, looking rather surprised at the silence.

His mother went over to the tea tray. He looked at her. 'Have you been crying, Mamma? You are so quiet.'

'We've been sitting here talking about a sad story, my young friend and I,' his mother said, indicating Ingrid.

'Oh, please forgive me,' he said. 'I did not notice that we had a visitor.'

The young girl stepped into the candlelight. She had all the beauty of one who knows that the gates of Heaven are about to open for her.

He greeted her rather stiffly, clearly without knowing who she was. His mother introduced her.

He gave Ingrid a fleeting glance.

'I saw Miss Berg down on the ice a little while ago,' he said.

He knew nothing about her, had never spoken to her before.

IX

Now there came a short period of happiness. Gunnar Hede had not been cured, that's true, but those closest to him were happy enough with the thought that he was on the road to health. Much of his memory was still missing and there were long periods of his life he had no idea about, nor could he play the fiddle. Almost everything he had ever learnt had vanished and his mental strength was so weak that he had no wish to read or to write. But for all that, he was much better. He was not frightened, he was fond of his mother and he had resumed the ways and habits of a gentleman. It was easy to see why his mother and the whole household were ecstatic.

Hede himself was in high spirits, full of joy and good cheer all day, never brooding, sliding easily past anything he could not understand, never talking about anything that demanded serious thought, but always conversing brightly and happily.

What gave him most pleasure was physical movement. He took Ingrid out tobogganing and ice skating. He did not say much to her but she enjoyed being allowed to go with him. He was friendly towards her as he was to everyone, but he was not in the least in love with her.

He frequently thought about his fiancée, wondering why she did not write or anything like that. But even that concern disappeared after a little while. He was quick to push aside any miserable thoughts.

It seemed to Ingrid that there was little chance of him recovering properly in this manner. At some point he would have to be forced to think, to look into himself in a way that he dared not do at present. But she would not take the risk of forcing him and nor would anyone else. If only he would fall in love with her just a little, she thought, then she would take the risk.

She believed that what they all needed to begin with was a little happiness.

*

At about this time a small child died at the manse in Råglanda where Ingrid had been fostered and it was necessary for the gravedigger to dig a grave to receive her.

The man dug the grave very close to where he had opened a grave for Ingrid the summer before and when he had dug down several feet he accidentally uncovered a corner of her coffin.

The gravedigger could not help smiling to himself a little. He had, of course, heard that the corpse in that coffin was said to have appeared as a ghost. On the very day of her funeral – supposedly – she had managed to unscrew the lid of the coffin, rise from the grave and show herself at the manse. Since the minister's wife was not that well-liked the parishioners had enjoyed hearing that sort of gossip about her.

If only, the gravedigger thought, if only people knew how securely buried the dead were in this earth and how well the coffin lids …

He had to stop mid-thought at that point. On the corner of the coffin he had just uncovered, the lid lay just a little squint and there was a screw that was not screwed home.

He said nothing, nor did he think anything, but for a while he stopped digging and whistled his way through the whole of the Värmland Regiment reveille, for he was an old soldier.

Then he thought that the best thing to do was to work his way through this business sensibly. It was not right for a gravedigger to entertain thoughts of the dead rising and doing as they pleased during the dark nights of autumn. So he quickly dug away more soil and began to hammer on the coffin with his shovel.

The coffin answered quite, quite clearly that it was empty,

empty, empty.

Half an hour later the gravedigger was standing in the manse, where a great deal of guessing and wondering ensued. One thing they all now realised was that the girl had been in the pedlar's sack. But where had she gone afterwards?

Since it was time to do the baking for another funeral meal, old Anna Stina was in the manse, standing by the baking oven attending to the loaves. She stood and listened at length to all this talk without saying a thing. She simply carried on keeping an eye on the baking so that it did not burn. She was continually putting trays in and taking trays out and it was dangerous to get too close to her because of the long oven-shovel she was using. But then, all of a sudden, she took off her kitchen apron, wiped as much of the sweat and soot from her face as she could and found herself standing before the minister almost before she knew it.

As a result of all this it was hardly surprising that on one day in March the small red manse sledge, painted with green tulips and pulled by a little red manse horse, should draw up at the front steps of Munkhyttan.

And, of course, Ingrid now had to return home to her mother. The minister had come to collect her. He did not say a great deal about how glad they were that she was alive and so on, but you could see that he was really pleased. He had never been able to forgive himself for them not being kind enough to their foster-daughter and he beamed with joy at the chance to start anew and to do it right this time.

Not a word was said about why she had run away. There was nothing to be gained from digging all that up and tormenting themselves with it after all this time. But Ingrid was given to understand that the minister's wife had been through a difficult period, having been conscience-stricken, and now they wanted Ingrid back so that they could be kind to her. She understood that she was almost under an obligation to go to the manse in order to show that she did not hold a grudge against her foster-parents.

Everyone thought it natural that she should go home for a week or two. And why not? She could not make any excuses about being needed where she was. It was obvious, of course, that she could be away for a few weeks without any harm coming to Gunnar Hede. It was not easy for her, but it was probably all for the best, given that everyone thought she should go.

It may well have been that she was hoping they would ask her to stay. She took her seat in the sledge thinking that the inspector's widow or Stava the housekeeper would come and lift her out of it and carry her indoors. She found it quite impossible to imagine herself riding down the avenue, travelling out into the forest and seeing Munkhyttan disappear behind her.

Perhaps it was out of kindness that they did not want to stop her leaving. They might well have been thinking that, what with her youth and love of life, she would want to get away from the isolation of Munkhyttan. They might well have been thinking that she had tired of being the madman's guardian. She raised her hand, wanting to grasp the reins and turn the horse. It was only then, half a dozen miles from the manor, that it occurred to her that that was the reason they had let her go and she would have liked to turn back and ask them.

The great silence that now closed around her left her wandering astray in a trackless forest: not a single human being offered her an answer or advice, nor was an answer to be heard from the pines and the spruces, from the squirrel and the eagle owl.

*

It made little difference how they treated her back at the manse. She believed she was being very well treated but, in truth, it made little difference. Nor would it have made any difference if she had been in a castle or an enchanted paradise garden. There is no bed soft enough to bring comfort to a yearning soul.

At first she asked as humbly as possible every day to be allowed to return now that she had had the great joy of seeing her mother and brothers and sisters once more. But the state of the roads made it quite out of the question, she could see that, couldn't she? She would have to be patient until the ground thawed out. And returning to that place surely wasn't a matter of life and death, was it?

Ingrid found it hard to understand why people became angry when she said she wanted to return to the Hede family. Father and mother and everyone else in the parish reacted in the same way: it seemed that when you were in Råglanda you weren't allowed to want to be anywhere else in the world.

She soon found that it was best not to mention anything at all about going back. If she did refer to it, any number of objections would immediately be found. It was not enough that the road was still in a very poor state, they surrounded her with fences and walls and moats. There were quilts for her to make, cloth for her to weave, plants to be planted in the cold-frame. And surely she didn't want to leave before the big birthday celebration at the manse? And she wasn't going to leave before Karin Landberg's wedding, was she?

There was nothing left for her to do but to raise her hands to the spring sky and pray for it to hurry up with its work. Just to pray for sunshine and warmth, to beg the kindly sun to work on the forest and aim the heat of its little sunbeams down between the spruce trees and melt the snow beneath them. Dear Heavens, it didn't matter whether the snow in the valley melted, just as long as the hills were clear, as long as the forest tracks were passable, as long as the farm girls could return to the shielings, as long as the bogs dried up, as long as the shorter road was clear – the road that was only half the distance of the highway.

And once the forest track was passable Ingrid knew who would not be waiting for transport or humbly begging for travel money. She knew who would slip away from the manse one clear night, knew who would do so without asking permission from anyone.

In years past Ingrid had thought she knew what waiting for spring was – waiting for spring, after all, was something everyone did. But now Ingrid realised she had never yearned for spring before. Oh no, what she had felt before could not be called yearning!

In the past she had waited for green leaves and anemones, for the song of the thrush and the call of the cuckoo. But those were just childish things, no more than that. You were not truly yearning for spring if you only thought of the pretty things. What you should do is pick up and kiss the first clump of earth that pokes through the snow, pluck the first wrinkled nettle leaf and let it burn the coming of spring into your skin.

Everyone was being so unbelievably kind to her, but although she never mentioned it they all knew that the thought of leaving was always in her mind.

'I cannot understand why you want to go back to that place and look after that mad fellow,' Karin Landberg said one day. It was as if she could read Ingrid's mind.

'Oh, she's put that out of her mind now,' the minister's wife said before the girl herself had time to answer.

When Karin had gone the minister's wife said: 'People do wonder why you want to leave us.'

Ingrid said nothing.

'People are saying that you may have fallen in love with Hede after he recovered.'

'Oh no, not after,' Ingrid said, feeling a desire to laugh.

'Anyway, he can't be worth marrying,' her foster-mother said. 'Father and I have talked about it and we think it's best you stay here with us.'

'It's kind of you to want me here,' Ingrid said. And she really was touched that they wanted to be so kind to her.

But however submissive she became they still did not trust her and she had no way of knowing in which star they read her longing. Even though they had just told her that she could not go back her foster-mother would not let the subject drop.

'They would, of course, write if they needed you there,' she said.

Once again Ingrid felt an urge to laugh. The arrival of a letter from an enchanted castle would be quite the strangest thing in the world and she wondered whether her foster-mother really believed that the King of the Mountain Hall would write requesting the return of the spell-bound maiden who had stayed too long with her mother.

If her foster-mother had any idea how many messages she actually received, it would have made her head spin.

Messages came in her dreams at night and they came in her visions in the day. He was telling Ingrid that he needed her, that he was ill, so ill.

She knew he was going mad again and that she must go to him. If anyone had told her this her immediate response would have been that she already knew.

Those great starry eyes of hers gazed farther and farther into the distance. Anyone looking into her eyes would find it hard to believe that she was likely to remain calmly and quietly at the manse.

It is not really difficult to see whether someone is happy or whether she is longing for something. You only need to see the little spark of joy in her eyes when she comes in from work or when she sits down by the fire. And there was no spark of joy in Ingrid's eyes except when she saw the mountain burn come dancing out of the forest and overflowing its banks, for it was the burn that was clearing the path for her.

There was one occasion when Ingrid was with Karin Landberg and began telling her about her life at Munkhyttan. Karin had been quite frightened. How had Ingrid been able to bear such things?

Karin Landberg was soon to be married and had reached the stage where she could talk of nothing but her fiancé. She knew nothing unless he had taught it to her and she would do nothing without asking him first.

Karin recalled that Olof had told her something about this Gunnar Hede business, something she felt she could use to frighten Ingrid from growing too fond of the madman. And so she started to tell her how mad the fellow really had been. Olof had told her that at market last autumn he had heard a couple of men say that Billy Goat was not mad at all. He simply pretended to be mad in order to attract customers. But Olof had insisted that he was crazy and to prove it he had gone to the animal pen and bought a worthless little goat.

All Olof then had to do was to stand the goat on the counter where the madman had laid out all his knives and the fellow had run away from his pack and from his wares. Everyone present doubled up with laughter to see how frightened he was. Surely Ingrid could not care for someone as mad as that, it just wasn't possible.

Karin Landberg should perhaps have paid more attention to Ingrid's face while she was telling this story. Had she done so she would perhaps have noticed the way she knitted her brows, would perhaps have seen the warning signs.

'And you still want to marry a man who could behave like that, do you?' Ingrid said. 'I think it would be better to marry the Billy Goat himself!'

Ingrid said this and quite clearly she meant it. It was unusual for Ingrid, who was so gentle, to say something so harsh that it cut Karin to the quick. Karin worried for days afterwards that Olof was not the man she wanted him to be. It made her life bitter until she plucked up courage and talked to him about it, and he was kind and loving enough to calm her fears and comfort her.

Waiting for spring is not an easy thing to do in Värmland. It might be sunny and warm in the evening but the ground can still be white with snow the following morning. The gooseberry bushes and the lawns might be green but the birchwoods remain bare and stubbornly refuse to come into leaf.

By Whitsun spring had come to the valley, but Ingrid's prayers were still not being answered: the farm girls had not moved to the shielings, the bogs had not dried out, and there was no hope of getting through on the forest track.

Ingrid was in church on Whit Sunday, as was her foster-mother. It was such an important day that they went there in the carriage. In the past Ingrid had always enjoyed arriving at the church at full speed and seeing the people standing by the stone wall and along the roadside doff their caps in greeting, while all those standing in the road leapt aside with a couple of bounds. But nothing gave her pleasure any longer. 'Longing can rob the rose of its scent and the full moon of its gleam,' as the proverb says.

But Ingrid liked what she heard in the church. It was good to hear that a miracle of joy had comforted the disciples in their longing. She liked this, she liked the thought of Jesus comforting those who were beside themselves with longing for him.

While Ingrid and all the others were in church a tall man from Dalarna came walking down the road. He was wearing a sheepskin coat and carrying a heavy pack of wares on his back, like a man who cannot tell whether it is summer or winter, weekday or holy day. He did not enter the church and he crept very cautiously past the horses that were tethered along the verge close to the churchyard.

Once there he sat down on a grave and thought of all the dead people who were still sleeping and also of one who had woken and come to life. He was still sitting there when people began to come out of church.

Karin Landberg's Olof was one of the first to come out and when he glanced over towards the churchyard he caught sight of the man from Dalarna. It is difficult to say whether it was curiosity or something else that led him to go over to talk to him. He wanted to find out whether it was possible for the man to have gone mad again after he was supposed to have been cured.

And perhaps it was true. The pedlar told the young man that he was sitting there waiting for someone called Grave-Lily. She was going to come and play for him. She could play so that the sun danced and the stars ran in rings.

That was when Karin Landberg's Olof told him that the person he was waiting for was standing outside the church. He only needed to stand up and he would be able to see her. And she would undoubtedly be glad to meet him.

The minister's wife and Ingrid were just climbing into the carriage when a tall Dalarna man hurried towards them. He was moving quite quickly in spite of having to bob to all the horses, and he was waving his hand eagerly to the young girl.

As soon as Ingrid caught sight of him she stopped and stood still. She would not have been able to say whether what she felt most was joy at seeing him or despair at him having lost his mind again, but she forgot everything else in the world.

And her eyes began to shine. At that moment there can be no doubt that she saw nothing of the poor pathetic human creature and felt only the presence of the noble soul she had become ill longing for.

All the church-goers were standing around and were unable to resist looking. Not one of them could take their eyes from her face. She did not move and go towards him, she just stood and waited for him. But those who saw her glow with happiness might easily have assumed that it was some great and grand figure approaching her rather than a madman.

They said afterwards that there seemed to be a bond between his soul and her soul, a secret bond lying so far below the conscious level that human reason could not reach it.

But when Hede was only a few steps away from Ingrid her foster-mother quickly grabbed her, lifted her up and put her in the carriage. She did not want there to be a meeting between the two of them in full view of everyone outside the church. And the moment they were in the carriage the farm-hand set the horses off at a gallop.

They heard wild and dreadful cries behind them and the minister's wife thanked God that she had managed to get the girl into the carriage.

Just a little later in the afternoon a farmer arrived at the manse to speak to the minister. He had come to talk to him about the madman from Dalarna, who was now raving so much that they had been forced to tie him up. What did the minister advise? What were they to do with him?

The only advice the minister had for them was that they should take him home. He told the farmer who the madman was and where he lived.

Later in the evening he told Ingrid, thinking it wisest to let her know the truth so that she might be guided by her own good sense.

When night fell Ingrid realised that she no longer had time

to wait for spring. She set off, poor lass, to walk the high road to Munkhyttan. She knew she would get there eventually, though she also knew it was twice as far as by the forest tracks.

X

It was the afternoon of Whit Monday and Ingrid was walking along the high road through a light open district of small low hills with little islands of birch trees between and sometimes out in the middle of the fields. The rowan and the bird-cherry were in flower, there were light, sticky leaves on the aspen trees and the ditches beside the road were rippling and full of clear water that made the newly washed stones at the bottom glisten and gleam.

As Ingrid walked she was grieving for Hede, who had lost his mind again. She was wondering whether there was anything she could do for him, whether there was anything to be gained by setting off from home like this.

Hungry and tired and with her shoes beginning to fall apart she wondered whether it might be better to turn back. It seemed unlikely that she would ever reach Munkhyttan.

The farther she went the more despondent she became. She could not help thinking that there was little point in going on when Hede was so completely mad. It was surely too late now and things had become hopeless.

But whenever she considered turning back she saw Hede's face cheek to cheek with her own as she had seen it so often before. It filled her with renewed hope. She thought he was calling to her and that brought her the comfort and the certainty that she would be able to heal him. Of course she could.

At that very moment Ingrid raised her head and now, looking rather less downcast, she encountered a strange little party of people.

First there came a small horse pulling a small cart in which there sat a fat lady. Walking beside it was a thin worn-looking man with long moustaches.

Out here in the countryside where there was no one who understood Art, Herr and Fru Blomgren always made a point of looking like ordinary townsfolk. The little cart in which they drove around was well-covered and no one would have suspected that it contained nothing but fireworks and conjuring apparatus and the marionettes for a puppet theatre.

And no one would possibly have suspected that the fat old lady sitting on top of the load looking like a well-to-do townswoman had once been the Miss Violet who used to fly through the air, or that the man with the look of a pensioned-off soldier walking alongside was none other than Herr Blomgren. In order to relieve the monotony of the journey he would sometimes somersault over the horse or drive the thrushes and siskins in the roadside trees mad by throwing his voice in imitation of their song.

The horse was a tiny little beast which had formerly been used to turn a carousel and consequently refused to move unless it heard music. That was why Fru Blomgren usually sat on top of the cart playing a mouth-organ, which she would quickly put in her pocket as soon as they met anyone; they did not want people thinking they were itinerant entertainers of the sort generally held in contempt. As a result of this their progress was not particularly rapid, but on the other hand they were in no great hurry to get anywhere anyway.

They made the blind fiddler walk a short distance behind everyone else so that passers-by would not suspect he belonged to their party. The blind man had a little dog to guide him. They would not allow him to be led by a child because that would have been a constant reminder to Herr and Fru Blomgren of a little girl called Ingrid. That would have been much too painful.

But now it was spring and so they had come out into the country. However good the earnings might be in town, Herr and Fru Blomgren simply had to move out and tour the countryside at this time of year. They were, after all, artistes, Herr and Fru Blomgren.

They did not recognise Ingrid and at first she walked past them without even saying hello, for she was in a hurry and was frightened of being held up. But then she thought she was being heartless and rude, so she turned back.

If there was anything in the world that could have made Ingrid happy at that point it was to witness the joy the old people showed on meeting her. And a long conversation ensued, all in almost incomprehensible double Dutch. Time after time the little horse turned round to see if the carousel had broken down.

Strangely enough it was Ingrid who did most of the talking. The old couple had, of course, noticed she had been weeping as she walked and they were so worried that they made her give a full account of everything that had happened to her.

And it was a great relief for Ingrid to be able to tell them, for these old people had their own way of taking things. They clapped their hands when they heard how she had risen from the grave and when she told them how she had frightened the minister's wife.

They patted her and praised her for leaving the manse. To them nothing was burdensome and troublesome, everything was easy and hopeful.

They had no measure by which they could judge reality because they themselves were beyond reach of its harshness, so they compared everything they heard to their marionette plays and pantomimes. There is always a little sorrow and unhappiness in pantomimes, everyone knows that, but they are only there to heighten the effect. And, of course, there is always a happy ending. Pantomimes always end well.

There was something infectious about all this hopefulness. Ingrid knew that they simply did not understand how great her unhappiness was, but it was encouraging to hear them, for all that.

And they were a great help in another way. They told her they had eaten dinner at the inn at Torsåker just a little while before and as they were finishing their meal some farmers arrived at the inn with a madman. Fru Blomgren could not bear madmen and had therefore wanted to leave immediately. Herr Blomgren had, of course, obeyed her. But what if that man had been Ingrid's madman? No sooner did they suggest this than Ingrid said it was more than likely to have been him, and she wanted to set off at once.

Then, in his usual ceremonious way, Herr Blomgren asked his wife whether they were on the road solely because it was spring and whether it made any difference to them in which direction they travelled; and old Fru Blomgren responded in tones equally lofty, asking whether he imagined for one moment she would think of deserting their dear Ingrid before she had reached a haven of happiness.

So the carousel horse was turned round and conversation became rather more difficult because it was time to play the mouth organ again. Whenever Fru Blomgren wanted to say something she had to pass the instrument to Herr Blomgren and when Herr Blomgren wanted to speak he had to pass it back to his wife. And the little horse came to a halt whenever the mouth organ was passing from mouth to mouth.

They spent the whole time telling Ingrid one comforting story after another. They went through all the stories they had seen played in the puppet theatre. They comforted her with Sleeping Beauty, they comforted her with Cinderella, they comforted her with all the fairy tales in the world.

Herr and Fru Blomgren watched Ingrid and they saw how her eyes began to light up just a little.

'The eyes of an artiste!' they said, nodding to one another in satisfaction. 'What was it we said? The eyes of an artiste!'

In some unfathomable way they had discovered that Ingrid had become one of their own, one of the artistes. They thought of her as playing a role in a drama. It was a triumph for them in their old age.

They travelled as quickly as they could. The only thing worrying the old couple was whether Ingrid's madman would still be at the inn.

But he was still there and, what was worse, no one knew how to take him on from there.

The two Råglanda farmers who had come with him had put him in one of the rooms at the inn and locked him in while they waited for horses. His hands had been securely tied behind his back when they left him, but somehow he had managed to twist his hands loose from the rope so that when they came to fetch him he had been standing there free and in such a rage that he had grabbed a chair to use as a weapon. They'd had no choice but to get out quickly and bar the door behind them. The farmers were now waiting for the innkeeper and his men to arrive back so that there would be enough of them to tie up the madman again.

The flame of hope her old friends had kindled in Ingrid did not, however, flicker out. She realised that Hede was worse than ever, but she had not expected anything else. In spite of everything, she was still hopeful. It was not so much their stories that had raised her spirits, it was the great love they had shown her.

She asked to be allowed to go in to Hede. She said she knew him and he would do her no harm. But the farmers answered that, unlike him, they were not mad: that fellow would kill anyone who went in.

Ingrid sat in silent thought for a long time. She thought how strange it was that she had met Herr and Fru Blomgren on that day of all days. There must surely be some reason for it? Their paths would not have crossed unless there was a reason.

And she began thinking about what had led to Hede's recovery the last time. Could she once again find something that would remind him of the old days, something that would lead him away from the thoughts of a madman? She thought and thought.

*

Herr and Fru Blomgren were sitting on a bench outside the inn looking unhappier than anyone thought possible. They were on the verge of tears.

Ingrid, the dear child, came over to them and smiled at them in the way that only she could; she stroked their furrowed old cheeks and begged them to give her the great joy of watching them perform as she had seen them do every day in the past. It would bring her so much comfort.

At first they said no, for they could hardly be said to be in their customary happy artiste mood, could they? But when she bestowed several more smiles on them they could not resist her and went out to the cart and unpacked their costumes.

When they were ready, and when the blind fiddler had been summoned, Ingrid chose the location for the performance. She did not want them to perform in the courtyard, but the inn had a garden and she led them there. The garden consisted mostly of bare beds in which nothing had come up yet, but here and there stood apple trees in flower. Ingrid said that she wanted them to perform beneath one of these flowering apple trees.

They even had a small audience since farmhands and servant girls came running up as soon as they heard the fiddle. But Herr and Fru Blomgren were very downcast and it went against the grain for them to perform in that mood. Ingrid, much as they loved her, was asking too much of them.

It was unfortunate that Ingrid had taken them round to the garden side of the building, for that was the direction the guest-room windows faced. It was obvious she had not taken this into consideration and Fru Blomgren was on the point of running away when she heard one of the windows being thrown open. What if the madman had heard the music and what if he jumped out through the window and came down among them?

But Fru Blomgren regained her composure when she saw the man standing in the window. He was a young man of pleasant appearance, in his shirtsleeves but otherwise properly dressed. There was a calm look in his eyes, a slight smile on his lips and he was pushing his hair back from his forehead with his hand.

Herr Blomgren was working hard and so involved in the performance that he did not notice anything. Fru Blomgren, who had nothing to do beyond blowing kisses, could pay attention to everything.

Was it not amazing how Ingrid, the dear child, had

suddenly lit up? Her eyes shone as never before and her face gleamed with a pale light. And the force of all this brightness was directed at the man standing in the window.

The man did not hesitate for long before stepping up onto the window ledge and jumping down to them. He walked straight up to the blind man and asked if he might borrow his fiddle.

Ingrid immediately took the fiddle from the blind man and passed it to the stranger. 'Now we'll have the waltz from *Der Freischütz*,' she said.

The stranger began to play and Ingrid smiled, but there was something so far beyond ordinary nature about her that Fru Blomgren thought the girl would dissolve into a ray of sunshine and disappear.

And when Fru Blomgren heard the stranger play she recognised who he was. 'Aha,' she said to herself. 'Aha. So that's who it is. So that's why she wanted to see us old people perform.'

*

Gunnar Hede, who had entered the room at the inn in such a rage that he felt like killing someone, had heard a blind man playing outside the window. The sound had taken him back to a scene in his past life.

He began wondering where his own fiddle was and he remembered that Ålin had taken it away, which left him with no choice but to try to borrow the blind man's fiddle in order to play himself to peace. He was so terribly upset.

As soon as he had the blind man's fiddle in his hands he began to play. It never occurred to him that he would not be able to play. He had no idea that for many years he had only been capable of playing a couple of small and simple tunes.

He was quite convinced that he was standing outside the Uppsala house with the Virginia creeper and waiting for the performers to start dancing as they had done last time.

Hede tried to put more spirit into his playing to encourage them to join in, but his fingers were stiff and reluctant and the bow refused to obey him properly. He went at it so hard that drops of sweat broke out on his forehead. Eventually he arrived at the right melody, the one they had danced to the last time, and now he played it so seductively, so enticingly that it would melt the hearts of those who heard it.

But the old acrobats did not start dancing. It was so long since they had met Hede in Uppsala that they could not remember how they had been swept away at that time and they had no idea what he was expecting of them.

Hede turned towards Ingrid for an explanation of why the performers were not dancing. But the moment he caught sight of her eyes and of the heavenly brightness that shone from them he was so astonished that he stopped playing.

He stood for a moment looking at the circle of people around him. All of them were watching him, their eyes wondering and uneasy.

He found it impossible to play with people staring like that and he simply walked away from them. He could see a group of flowering apple trees down in the garden and that was where he went.

It was clear to him now that none of this matched the thought he had entertained a moment ago, that he was in Uppsala and that Ålin had shut him in. This garden was too big and the house was not covered with the red leaves of Virginia creeper. This could not be Uppsala, then.

But he was not especially concerned about where he was. He felt as though he had not played for centuries, but now he had got hold of a fiddle and now he was going to play!

He put the fiddle under his chin and he began. Once again the stiff movements of his fingers hindered him and he could play nothing but the simplest pieces.

'We're going to have to start again right from the beginning,' he said, and he smiled and began to play a little minuet, the first piece he had ever learned. Father played it first and he had followed, picking it up by ear. All at once he could see the whole scene and he could hear the words: 'The little prince should learn to dance, but he broke his little leg.'

Then he tried several little dance tunes, ones he had played as a schoolboy. He had been invited to visit the girls' school to play for their dancing classes. He could see in his mind the small girls hopping and turning and hear their dancing mistress beating time with her foot.

He began to be a little bolder. He played the first violin part of a string quartet by Mozart, which he had learnt at the grammar school in Falun. A quartet of old gentlemen had been practising for a concert and the first violin had been taken ill. He had to take over, young as he was, and he had been more than a little proud of himself.

The only thing in Gunnar Hede's mind as he played these childish exercises was getting his fingers to work properly. But he soon noticed that something wonderful was happening to him.

He recognised clearly that there was a great zone of darkness in his mind, blocking out the past. Whenever he tried to recall anything it was like searching in a darkened room. But now, with no conscious effort on his part, the darkness rolled back sufficiently for him to remember his childhood and schooldays.

He decided to let the fiddle lead him. Perhaps it would drive away the rest of the darkness.

And that is what happened. With every piece he played the darkness surrounding his past receded a little. The fiddle led him on year by year, wakening memories of his studies, of friends, of pleasures. The darkness before him was dense, but when he approached it armed with the fiddle it retreated step by step. Every so often he would look back as if to see whether the darkness was closing behind him. But behind him all was as clear as day.

The fiddle moved on to a series of duets to be played by violin and piano. He only played a few bars of each but the darkness moved back considerably and he remembered his fiancée and the time of their engagement.

He would have liked to dwell on that period, but there was still a great deal of darkness to be played away and he had no time to wait.

He came to a hymn tune. He had heard it once when he

had been sad. He remembered sitting in a country church and hearing it, but why had he been sad? Because by then he had been roaming the country with his wares as a poor pedlar. It was a hard way of life and his memories of it were sad.

The bow moved across the strings like a whirlwind and another great rent appeared in the curtain of darkness. This time he saw the vast forest, the animals buried in the snow, the strange shapes formed by the snow drifting over them. He remembered his visit to his fiancée and recalled how she had broken off their engagement. All of this suddenly became clear to him.

He felt neither joy nor sorrow at any of the things he remembered. The important thing was that he remembered them. That and that alone gave him infinite satisfaction.

After that the bow stopped as though of its own accord. It did not want to take him farther. And yet there was more, much more, that he had to remember. There was still a wall of darkness in front of him.

He forced the bow to continue. It played two inconsequential tunes, the tritest little tunes he had ever heard. How on earth had his bow learnt things like that?

The darkness did not recede an inch when these tunes were played. He learnt nothing at all from them, but what did emerge was a feeling of anxiety so great that he could not recall ever having experienced anything like it. A mad, horrifying terror, the dread irrational fear of souls that are doomed.

He stopped playing, unable to bear it. What was it that lay in these tunes? What was it?

The darkness did not retreat before them and the dreadful thing was that he felt that the moment he stopped advancing on the darkness and driving it away with the fiddle it came sweeping back and threatened to close around him.

He had been playing with half-closed eyes and now he opened his eyes and looked out into the world of reality. And he caught sight of Ingrid, who had been standing listening to him the whole time.

Without any expectation of an answer, but so as to hold

back the darkness for a moment, he asked her, 'When did I last play these things?'

Ingrid stood and trembled, but she had made her decision. Whatever happened he would now learn the truth. Whatever happened she would tell him the truth.

Fearful she might be, but she was brave and utterly determined. He was not going to elude her now, she was not going to let him slip away from her.

But despite all her courage she did not dare tell Hede directly that these were the tunes he had played when he was mad. Instead, she circled around the question.

'These were the tunes you used to play when you were at home in Munkhyttan last winter,' she said.

Hede was surrounded by mysteries. Why did this girl address him with the familiar form *du*? She was not one of the ordinary country people – she wore her hair up and curled into small ringlets in the manner of gentlefolk. Her dress was homespun but she had a fichu of fine lace at her throat. Her complexion was white and her hands small. It seemed quite out of the question that a peasant girl could have features so refined and such large dreaming eyes. Hede's memory could tell him nothing about her. Why did she say *du* to him? And how could she know that he had played these things at his home?

'What is your name?' he asked. 'Who are you?'

'I am Ingrid,' she said, 'whom you saw in Uppsala many years ago – the girl you comforted because she couldn't learn how to walk the tightrope.'

That memory lay in the part of the past that had already become clear to Hede and he could remember her well.

'How tall and beautiful you've become, Ingrid,' he said, 'and so grand! What a wonderful brooch!' He had been looking at her brooch for a long time. He thought he recognised it – it was very like an enamel and pearl brooch his mother owned.

The girl answered him immediately: 'You will certainly have seen it before. This brooch was given to me by your mother.'

Gunnar Hede put the fiddle down and came over to Ingrid. He asked her in a very forceful voice:

'How can you possibly be wearing her brooch? Why don't I know about you knowing my mother?'

Ingrid became ashen-faced with fear. She already knew what the next question would be.

'I don't know anything, Ingrid. I don't know why I'm here. I don't know why you are here. Why don't I know?'

'Don't ask me! Please don't ask me!' She stepped back and raised her hands as if to protect herself.

'Won't you tell me?'

'Don't ask! Don't ask!'

He gripped her wrist hard to force the truth from her. 'Just say it. I'm in full control of my senses. Why are there things I don't remember?'

She could see something wild and threatening in his eyes. He already knew what she was going to say to him, but she knew it was quite impossible to tell someone they had been mad. It was much more difficult than she had thought. It was impossible, impossible.

'Say it!' he repeated. But she could hear from his voice that he did not want to hear it. He might even kill her if she said it.

Then she summoned all of her love and looked Gunnar Hede straight in the eye and said:

'You have not really been right in the head.'

'Not for a long time, perhaps?'

'I don't know exactly. Not for three or four years …'

'Raving mad, you mean?'

'No, no, not that! You've been able to buy and sell and work the markets.'

'In what way was I mad then?'

'You were afraid.'

'Afraid of what?

'Of animals …'

'Of goats, perhaps?'

'Yes, mostly of goats.'

Hede had kept a tight hold of her wrist the whole time, but now he threw her hand away from him. Really threw it. He turned from Ingrid in a violent rage, as though she had told him something slanderous with malice in mind.

But that emotion gave way to another, one which upset him even more deeply. He saw in front of him, as clearly as if he had been looking at a painting, a tall man from Dalarna, his back bent under the weight of an enormous pack. He wants to go into a farm cottage, but a pathetic little dog comes out and approaches him. He stops and bobs and bobs and is afraid to enter until a laughing man comes out of the cottage and chases the dog away.

When Hede saw this the terrible fear came back to him.

The vision disappeared, but voices came instead. People screaming and shouting around him. People laughing. Words of abuse, loud, close to him. Shrill children's voices shrieking – the most horrible and cruel of all. Words, a name that is repeated, screamed, shouted, whispered, hissed into his ear: Billy Goat, Billy Goat.

And all this was directed at him, at Gunnar Hede. This was what he had lived through. Even though now in full possession of his senses he felt the same unspeakable fear he had suffered as a madman. But it was no longer fear of something external, now he was afraid of himself.

'This is what I am. This is what I have been,' he said, twisting his hands. The next moment he was down on his knees bending forward over a small bench and weeping, weeping.

'And this is what I have been,' he wailed between the sobs. 'This is what I have been.'

Would he have the courage to bear that thought – the thought that he had been a broken and ridiculed madman? 'Oh, let me be mad again!' he said, striking the bench hard. 'It's more than anyone can bear!'

He held his breath for a moment. The darkness was approaching again, bringing him the salvation he had called for. It was sweeping towards him, moving like a bank of mist. A smile came to his lips. He could feel his features becoming slack, his eyes becoming the eyes of a madman again.

This was better. The other was not to be tolerated, was beyond endurance. Singled out, laughed at, mocked, mad! Better to be mad again and know nothing of it. What was the point of returning to the world to be loathed by everyone?

The first mist-like fingers of the veil of darkness began to close around him.

Ingrid stood there, seeing and hearing his fear and knowing only that everything would soon be lost again. She saw clearly that madness was taking hold of him once more.

And she was terrified, all her courage gone. But she wanted at least to bid farewell to him and to her own happiness before madness seized him and filled him with so much fear that no one could approach him.

Hede sensed Ingrid coming over to him, then falling to her knees beside him, putting her arm around his neck, her cheek to his cheek and kissing him.

She did not consider herself too good to approach him, madman that he was, she did not consider herself too good to kiss him!

A faint hissing sound was audible in the darkness. The fluttering patches of mist shrank back and took the form of snakes' heads that had been ready to strike but were now hissing in rage at being unable to bite.

'Don't take it so badly,' Ingrid said, 'don't take it so badly. As long as you get well no one will think of the past.'

'I want to go mad again,' he said. 'I can't bear this. I can't endure thinking of the way I was.'

'Of course you can,' Ingrid said.

'No one will forget it,' he wailed. 'I was so monstrous. No one can like me.'

'I like you.'

He looked up doubtfully. 'You only kissed me to stop me going mad again. You have sympathy for me.'

'I can easily kiss you again. I can,' she said.

'You are just saying that now because it's what I need to hear.'

'Do you need to hear that someone likes you?'

'Do I? My God, how I need to hear it! But, my child,' he said, pulling away from her, 'how can I ever live with the knowledge that all the people who see me will immediately think "There's the fellow who was mad. The one who went round bobbing to dogs and cats."'

He was overwhelmed by emotion again and lay and wept, head in his hands.

'Better to be mad again! I can hear them shouting at me and I can see myself. Fear, nothing but fear. Fear.'

That was when Ingrid lost patience.

'You are right,' she shouted. 'Just go mad again, go on! Going mad just to avoid a little fear, what a truly manly thing to do that is!'

She bit her lip, fighting back tears, and when she could not bring her words out fast enough she took hold of his arms and shook him.

She was furious, beside herself with anger because, with his refusal to struggle and fight, he was trying to escape her once again.

'What do you care about me? What do you care about your mother? Go on, go mad – then you'll have a peaceful life!'

She shook him again.

'To escape fear, you say. But you don't have any fears on behalf of someone who has spent the whole of her life waiting for you – and you never came! If your heart had feelings for anyone but yourself you could easily do battle with your demons and get well. But you have no heart for anyone else.

'In my dreams and visions you appear and beg for help so sweetly and movingly, but in reality you don't want help. You delude yourself that there is no suffering in the world worse than yours. But there certainly is, and there are people who have suffered far worse than you.'

Hede looked up at last and looked her straight in the eye. She was far from beautiful at that moment. Tears were pouring down her face and her lips quivered as she struggled to bring out her words between the sobs.

But it was good and right for him to see her so upset and a strange calm came over him, together with an overwhelming sense of humble gratitude. Something great and wonderful had reached out to him in the moment of his degradation. This must be great love, truly great love.

He had been lamenting his wretchedness, but love had come and was demanding to be allowed in. Nor was it just a case of being tolerated if he returned to life, of people managing to resist laughing at him.

There really was someone who loved him, who yearned for him. She was speaking harshly, but he heard love trembling in every word she spoke. He felt she was offering him kingdoms and thrones.

She told him he had been her salvation when he was a madman. He had wakened her from the dead, carried her and protected her. But that was not enough for her: she wanted him for her own.

When she had kissed him he had felt sweet balm on his sick soul, but he had not dared believe it was love that drove her. But her rage and her tears left him in no doubt. He was loved, poor monster, poor wretched creature that he was.

In the face of the great and humble bliss that this brought to him the last of the darkness retreated. It moved aside like a heavy rattling curtain and he could see the vale of terror through which he had walked. But it was in that vale he had met Ingrid, raised her from her grave, played for her in the cottage in the forest, and it was in that vale she had worked to heal him.

Not only did his memories of her return, but the feelings she had then aroused in him were reawakened. Love coursed through his whole being. He felt the same burning desire as he had felt outside the church at Råglanda when she had been snatched away from him.

A flower had grown in the realm of terror, in the great wasteland, and that flower comforted him with its beauty and its fragrance. And now he understood how love had become eternal. The wild desert flower had been transplanted into the garden of life, where it took root, grew and flourished. And when he understood this he knew he was saved, that the darkness had met its master.

Ingrid had fallen silent. She was weary with the weariness that follows a heavy task, but she was also calm, with a sense of having performed her work in the best way. She knew that victory was in her hands.

Hede finally broke his silence.

'I promise you that I shall not give in,' he said.

'Thank you,' she said.

No more was said at that time.

Hede felt he could never tell her how much he loved her. It could not be told in words, it could only be shown through every day and every hour of life, for as long as life lasted.

Translator's Afterword

Selma Lagerlöf began work on the short novel or novella that was to become *En herrgårdssägen* (A Manor House Tale) in the spring of 1899. In a letter to Sophie Elkan (17.04.1899) Lagerlöf wrote: 'It is really strange how, all of its own accord, this story has become a reproduction of the folktale *La Belle et La Bête* – do you know it? I didn't notice myself until it was all written'. Writing to Elisabeth Grundtvig, one of her Danish translators, a fortnight later she mentioned that she had already sent the manuscript to her Danish publisher, but she also said that the text had been composed very quickly and that consequently she found it hard to evaluate it and would be grateful for any comments (01.05.1899). The same uncertainty was expressed in a number of other letters and in the middle of June, when the story was already being typeset, she wrote apologetically to her Swedish publisher Albert Bonnier, sending him a new first chapter, telling him that a new second chapter would come the next day and more would follow: 'It really is a nuisance, but the important thing after all is that the story should be as good as possible' (12.06.1899). The rewrite was substantial and the work appeared in the autumn of 1899.

*

Gunnar Hede is a young student at Uppsala University and more given to playing his fiddle than to studying. The family estate and manor house at Munkhyttan are in financial danger after the decline of its iron mines and Hede, following in the footsteps of his grandfather, the founder of the family fortunes, sets out as a travelling pedlar. He is successful, but after helplessly witnessing the death of his herd of goats in a blizzard he loses his mind and continues to roam the countryside as a frightened pedlar, only visiting his Munkhyttan home at Christmas.

While still a student he had met Ingrid, an orphan child who fell in love with him and has carried him in her memory ever since. Years later, when she is nineteen, she falls into a death-like coma as a result of her sense of being unwanted and unloved. Hede, now a mentally disturbed pedlar whom she does not recognise as her student, rescues her from her grave.

Ingrid now becomes the companion to Hede's mother at the manor house at Munkhyttan. When Hede comes for his annual visit Ingrid slowly comes to understand that the student and the madman are one and the same and from then on she devotes her life to helping him overcome his terrors and put the darkness of madness behind him. It is a heavy task, but one in which she succeeds: 'A flower had grown in the realm of terror, in the great wasteland, and that flower comforted him with its beauty and its fragrance. And now he understood how love had become eternal. The wild desert flower had been transplanted into the garden of life, where it took root, grew and flourished. And when he understood this he knew he was saved, that the darkness had met its master.'

A Manor House Tale is at one and the same time a complex psychological novel and a folk tale, a love story and a Gothic melodrama. It crosses genre boundaries and also, like many of Selma Lagerlöf's texts, locates itself in a borderland between reality and fantasy, madness and sanity, darkness and light, possession and loss, life and death. Her skill as an artist lies, among much else, in her ability to lead her reader seamlessly from the everyday through multiple modes of the 'other' and back to an everyday that is now enhanced by the victory of goodness and love. Her art (to paraphrase John Gardner) celebrates life's potential, offering a vision unmistakeably and unsentimentally rooted in love. Her hypotexts are many – the Beauty and the Beast of her initial version, the myth of Cupid and Psyche – but it is perhaps the myth of Orpheus and Eurydice that has most resonance, not least because of the role of music. Lagerlöf's myth, however, involves a double salvation: each of the protagonists, Ingrid and Gunnar, 'plays' the other back from a personal psychological underworld, and although both come close to repeating Orpheus's failure, neither does so.

*

Lagerlöf's writing and the moral force that underpins it has provided a stimulus found irresistible by artists in other fields. The quality and international reputation of early Swedish cinema, for instance, is due not least to the film adaptations of her work by the two outstanding film directors of the day, Victor Sjöström and Mauritz Stiller, and it may be claimed with some justification that the narrative vigour and emotional intensity of her texts and the filmed versions based on them contributed significantly to raising the status of film to a more respected art form.

A dozen of Selma Lagerlöf's works were turned into films during the silent era of Swedish cinema and in 1919 she signed a general agreement with the film company, Svenska Bio, giving them the film rights to her later books. The film of *En herrgårdssägen*, directed by Mauritz Stiller and bearing the title *Gunnar Hedes saga*, had its première at the start of 1923 – in the English-speaking world it was released variously as *The Blizzard* (USA) or as *Snowbound* or *The Judgement* (UK). It is one of three Lagerlöf films made by Stiller, and the plot differs quite radically from that of the novel. Cooperation with Stiller was less to Lagerlöf's taste than her work with Sjöström and when the script was submitted to her she was seriously displeased with it and withheld approval. She did not, however, make her objections public and the production went ahead. The publicity material for the film was careful to stress that it was a free adaptation: 'A film drama with themes drawn from Selma Lagerlöf's *Manor House Tale*, in a free adaptation and production by Mauritz Stiller'. The critical reception of Stiller's film was generally speaking notably positive as far as the story, the production and the acting went, but the majority of the critics also felt that it had few of the qualities they associated with Lagerlöf. After praising the film as entertaining and beautiful, the film critic of *Stockholms Dagblad* (02.01.1923), for example, went on to write that 'there is nothing of Selma Lagerlöf's story-telling in this film, not a trace of her delightful charm, not a breath of the old Värmland manor house, nor is there anything left of the foundation on which the tale is built.' The critic in *Svenska Dagbladet* (02.01.1923) went a step further: 'It is with a heavy heart that one notes that *Gunnar Hede's Saga* confirms the way that Swedish film is more and more moving away from the good old traditions of Swedish cinema. There is little of the spiritual force, the culture and the artistic purposefulness that made masterpieces of films such as *The Girl from the Marsh Croft, The Sons of Ingmar, Sir Arne's Treasure* and *The Phantom Carriage*. Instead, we can sense a worrying tendency to try to satisfy banal foreign tastes in film. It would be more than deplorable if considerations of practical finance were to lead to a devaluation of the strict artistic principles which have given Swedish cinema unique status in the international film market'. (Foreign tastes or not, it may be worth noting that Svenska Bio could find fewer foreign buyers for *Gunnar Hedes saga* than they had found for earlier Lagerlöf film adaptations.)

In addition to cinema, there have been numerous dramatisations of the novel for the theatre over the years. Particularly appropriate given the thematic importance of music in the story are a number of musical adaptations. The classical composer Jan Sandström was inspired to compose the orchestral suite *En herrgårdssägen* (1987) and in 1989 he was responsible for the score of the ballet of the same name created by Per Isberg and danced by the Royal Swedish Ballet as a recorded TV dance-drama. In a different musical style, the Värmland-based folk musician Magnus Stinnerbom composed the music for a dramatisation of *En herrgårdssägen* at the Västanå Theatre in Sunne in 2008.

The most recent – and rightly much praised – adaptation of the novel is the retelling of the story as a graphic novel by the artist Marcus Ivarsson: *Selma Lagerlöfs En herrgårdssägen,* published by Kartago förlag in 2013. (A sample chapter and introduction is available in *Swedish Book Review* and online.)

*

Since its publication in 1899 Lagerlöf's *En herrgårdssägen* has been translated into twenty-six languages, in many of which it has appeared in multiple editions over the years. The earliest translation was into Danish (1899), followed by Finnish and Dutch in 1900. Two separate German translations came out in 1901 (one in Germany, one in Austria) and the first English translation also arrived in 1901. Re-translations of the novel have been frequent: there have, for instance, been six German translations, three Portuguese, three English (including the present volume) and two in each of French, Spanish, Finnish, Dutch, Hungarian and Bulgarian. A new translation appeared in French as recently as 2001 and in Spanish in 2012.

The first English translation came in Jessie Bröchner's *From a Swedish Homestead* published in London by Heinemann in 1901. That volume contains *The Story of a Country House* (*En herrgårdssägen*) and *Queens at Kungahälla* (*Drottningar i Kungahälla*), along with ten short stories, some of which were drawn from Lagerlöf's 1894 collection *Osynliga länkar* (*Invisible Links*) and the rest would later appear in her 1904 collections *Legender* (*Legends*) and *Kristuslegender* (*Christ Legends*). This edition was republished by Doubleday, Page in New York in 1917 as vol. 8 in the Northland selection of Lagerlöf's works. The same translation was issued again by Books for Libraries Press, Freeport, N.Y., 1970. Jessie Bröchner was not a prolific translator: in addition to *From a Swedish Homestead* she translated Lagerlöf's *Jerusalem* (translation 1903) and two works from Danish; she was also the author of *Danish Life in Town and Country* (1903), one of a series of introductions to 'Our European Neighbours' published by G.P. Putnam in London and New York.

A second translation appeared in 1922. This was Claud Field's *The Tale of a Manor and Other Sketches*, published in London by T.W. Laurie, the 'other' contents being three short stories from the 1894 *Osynliga länkar* (*Invisible Links*): 'Roman Blood' (Romarblod), 'In Vineta' (I Vineta) and 'Tale Thott' (Tale Thott). Claud Field (1863-1941) was much more prolific all round. He was a Church Mission Society missionary in London and in Pakistan and Afghanistan for many years, wrote a number of books on missionary work and many volumes of oriental legends and wisdom, both authored and translated. In terms of Swedish translations, in addition to *The Tale of a Manor* he translated Lagerlöf's *Queens of Kungahälla* (London: T. W. Laurie, 1930) and seven volumes of August Strindberg between 1912 and 1922. He also translated several volumes from German and from Russian.

The present translation has been made from the first edition of *En herrgårdssägen* (Stockholm: Albert Bonniers förlag, 1899), accessed electronically through the Swedish Literature Bank (http://litteraturbanken.se). I am once again grateful to Helena Forsås-Scott for reading my translation with a careful eye and making many helpful suggestions along the way; thank you, too, to Sarah Death and to the team at Norvik Press.

Peter Graves

REFERENCES

Bergmann, Sven Arne, *Getabock och gravlilja: Selma Lagerlöfs En herrgårdssägen som konstnärlig text*. Göteborg: Skrifter utgivna vid Litteraturvetenskapliga institutionen vid Göteborgs universitet nr 30, 1997.

Gardner, John, *On Moral Fiction*. New York: Basic Books, 1978.

Toijer-Nilsson, Ying (ed.), *Selma Lagerlöf: Brev 1*. Lund: Gleerups, 1969.

Urbom, Ruth, 'Visualising a Classic', *Swedish Book Review* 2014:2, pp. 23-25.

Wivel, Henrik, *Snödrottningen: En bok om Selma Lagerlöf och kärleken*, tr. Birgit Edlund. Stockholm: Bonniers, 1990.

SELMA LAGERLÖF

The Löwensköld Ring

Charlotte Löwensköld

(translated by Linda Schenck)

The Löwensköld Ring (1925) is the first volume of the trilogy considered to have been Selma Lagerlöf's last work of prose fiction. Set in the Swedish province of Värmland in the eighteenth century, the narrative traces the consequences of the theft of General Löwensköld's ring from his coffin, and develops into a disturbing tale of revenge from beyond the grave. It is also a tale about decisive women. The narrative twists and the foregrounding of alternative interpretations confront the reader with a pervasive sense of ambiguity. *Charlotte Löwensköld* (1925) is the story of the following generations, a tale of psychological insight and social commentary, and of the complexities of a mother-son relationship. How we make our life 'choices' and what evil forces can be at play around us is beautifully and ironically depicted. The third volume, *Anna Svärd* (1928), is under preparation.

The Löwensköld Ring
ISBN 9781870041928
UK £9.95
(Paperback, 120 pages)

Charlotte Löwensköld
ISBN 9781909408067
UK £11.95
(Paperback, 290 pages)

SELMA LAGERLÖF

Nils Holgersson's Wonderful Journey through Sweden

(translated by Peter Graves)

Nils Holgersson's Wonderful Journey through Sweden (1906-07) is truly unique. Starting life as a commissioned school reader designed to present the geography of Sweden to nine-year-olds, it quickly won the international fame and popularity it still enjoys over a century later. The story of the naughty boy who climbs on the gander's back and is then carried the length of the country, learning both geography and good behaviour as he goes, has captivated adults and children alike, as well as inspiring film-makers and illustrators. The elegance of the present translation – the first full translation into English – is beautifully complemented by the illustrations specially created for the volume.

Nils Holgersson's Wonderful Journey through Sweden, Volume 1
ISBN 9781870041966
UK £12.95
(Paperback, 365 pages)

Nils Holgersson's Wonderful Journey through Sweden, Volume 2
ISBN 9781870041973
UK £12.95
(Paperback, 380 pages)

Nils Holgersson's Wonderful Journey through Sweden, The Complete Volume
ISBN 9781870041966
UK £29.95
(Hardback, 684 pages)

SELMA LAGERLÖF

The Phantom Carriage

(translated by Peter Graves)

Written in 1912, Selma Lagerlöf's *The Phantom Carriage* is a powerful combination of ghost story and social realism, partly played out among the slums and partly in the transitional sphere between life and death. The vengeful and alcoholic David Holm is led to atonement and salvation by the love of a dying Salvation Army slum sister under the guidance of the driver of the death-cart that gathers in the souls of the dying poor. Inspired by Charles Dickens's *A Christmas Carol*, *The Phantom Carriage* remained one of Lagerlöf's own favourites, and Victor Sjöström's 1920 film version of the story is one of the greatest achievements of the Swedish silent cinema.

The Phantom Carriage
ISBN 9781870041911
UK £11.95
(Paperback, 126 pages)

AUGUST STRINDBERG

The People of Hemsö

(translated by Peter Graves)

The People of Hemsö (1887) will come as a surprise to most English-language readers, used as they are to seeing the bitter controversialist of plays like *The Father* and *Miss Julie* or the seeker for cosmic meaning and reconciliation of those mysterious later dream plays *To Damascus* and *A Dream Play*. This novel, a tragicomic story of lust, love and death among the fishermen and farmers of the islands of the Stockholm archipelago, reveals a very different Strindberg. The vigour and humour of the narration, as well as its cinematic qualities, are such that we witness a great series of peopled panoramas in which place and time and character are somehow simultaneously specific and archetypical, and we leave the novel with memories of grand landscapes and spirited scenes.

In a recent essay Ludvig Rasmusson wrote: 'For me, *The People of Hemsö* is the Great Swedish Novel, just as … *The Adventures of Huckleberry Finn* [is] the Great American Novel'. His comparison is an apt one: if the Mississippi becomes the quintessence of America, the island of Hemsö and the archipelago become the quintessence of Sweden.

The People of Hemsö
ISBN 9781870041959
UK £11.95
(Paperback, 164 pages)

Lightning Source UK Ltd.
Milton Keynes UK
UKOW06f0416160915

258677UK00008B/116/P

9 781909 408258